Ran Like
Joseph

A novel by
Jimmy Deas

ISBN:9781795665636

DEDICATION

To my sisters, Angela, Cheryl, and Wendy and the memories we share and the memory of our mother who instilled in us a love of reading.

ACKNOWLEDGMENTS

Thanks to my sisters, Angela McDaniel and Cheryl McCall for proof reading and my friend, David Butler for his suggestions and encouragement

Chapter 1

It was a little after 8:00pm on an August night. The temperature was still over 80 degrees, made worse by the North Florida humidity. The Reverend Mark Thomas and his landlady, Edith Cole sat on the screened front porch, thankful for the breeze generated by a box fan. Without the screening, mosquitos would have made it almost impossible to sit outside. Occasionally one did get inside and required a quick slap to that portion of the body where it lit. During the two months he had lived in her apartment, he had grown fond of Mrs. Cole. A widow for five years, she had lived her entire fifty-eight years in Gentry, was a life-long member of the Baptist Church, and as postmistress, knew everyone in the northern end of the county and was an invaluable source of information for the new preacher. She was not a gossip but a quiet, unassuming woman who was respected and trusted by everyone in the little town.

As they talked, he heard a car stop at the traffic light, the only one in Gentry, Florida situated on US Highway 41. There wasn't much traffic on Highway 41 at night since the opening of Interstate 75. Must be a local, he thought. After the light turned green he heard the car begin to accelerate and move in the direction of the Cole house which was located four blocks south of the traffic light, called a red light by the locals. As the car came even with the house, it accelerated as most cars did when drivers saw the 45 miles per hour sign two blocks past the Cole house.

Just as the car passed by, there was a sound of screeching brakes, burning rubber and a loud thud. The car stopped and the driver jumped out, screaming, "NO! NO!" and ran to the front of the car. Thomas jumped up, pushed the screen door open, and sprinted the thirty yards to where the car had stopped with the motor still running. As he ran to the front of the car, he could see the driver, a middle-aged man, standing over a person lying in the middle of the road. The driver looked at Thomas and said, "I couldn't help it. I didn't see him." The man was in obvious distress, looking as if he would faint at any moment.

The person lying in the road was a young male and Mark could see he was severely injured. One leg was broken and turned out at an odd angle. He was sure there were internal injuries as well. Kneeling on the pavement, he gently placed a hand under the victim's head and lifted it so he could see in the headlights of the still running car. As he turned the head, he recognized Sammy Garber, a teenager who was a member of the Gentry Baptist Church where Mark was the pastor. Sammy groaned and Thomas put both knees on the pavement and cradled the boy's head. "Sammy, it's Reverend Thomas. What happened?" The teenager struggled to open his eyes. With obvious effort he said, "Ran." It seemed as if he tried to speak another word but paused and then he said, "Joseph." He then lapsed into unconsciousness.

People from both sides of the street were now coming out to see what had happened. Thomas yelled out, "Someone call Stump Harris." Harris was a local farmer who served as Gentry's part-time law enforcement officer. His duties mainly consisted of managing traffic for funeral processions and breaking up fights among drunks on the weekend at Mac's Bar. Gentry had little crime activity. The curious gathered around and started asking the expected questions. "What happened?" and "Who is it?" Such questions did not help the condition of the driver and he leaned over the hood of car for support. In a loud voice, Thomas said, "It's Sammy Garber. He ran out in front of this man's car."

There were startled expressions and a couple of muttered comments directed towards the distraught driver, but just then a green Mercury Comet came out of a side street and stopped crossways of the highway. Stump Harris jumped out and quickly came around the front of his car. In a no-nonsense voice, he asked "What happened?"

"It's Sammy Garber," Thomas said. "He ran out in front of this car. He's hurt but I can't tell how bad." Stump looked at Mrs. Cole standing on the sidewalk in front of her house. "Edith, call Carswell's and tell them we need the ambulance and hurry." The Carswell Funeral Home was in Tadlock, the county seat and the hearse served the county as an ambulance for emergencies. Harris approached the driver and asked him what happened. In a breaking voice, he recounted leaving the traffic light, accelerating his car, and then, without warning, the teenager had run out in front of his car. In a desperate tone, he said, "I couldn't stop. I never saw him. Honest."

Mark's knees began to ache from pressing against the hard pavement. He also became aware of something wet and sticky on his hands. Gently turning Sammy's head, he could see where a large section of scalp was torn away, and blood was oozing. His muscles were beginning to tighten up and he wondered how much longer he could stay in that position.

Mrs. Cole came down the sidewalk and said, "They can't come. The ambulance has gone to pick up a body and won't be back for at least an hour." Stump grunted. "Can't wait," he said. Turning, he walked back towards where Mark was holding Sammy. "Preacher, I can be in Tadlock in fifteen minutes. We'll put him in the back seat. You can hold him."

He turned to the crowd and called for two men to assist getting Sammy into the back seat of the Mercury. "Help the preacher and be careful. We don't how bad it is." He then asked Mrs. Cole to call the Sheriff and send a deputy to investigate the accident. "Mister, you go sit on her porch and wait for the deputy." The man nodded and slowly walked to the porch as if in a trance. If someone had told him to climb the town water tower and jump off, he probably would have done it. "Somebody go get Nell and bring her to the hospital." With that done, he went to his car where Sammy had been loaded into the back seat with Mark holding his head. The boy had groaned when he was lifted and placed in the car. His head rested on Mark's lap and the blood from his head wound began to slowly stain his khaki pants. At least they were an old pair, he thought.

Harris placed a red flashing light on the dash of the car and turned it on. He pulled away from the crowd of on-lookers and quickly picked up speed. Mark could not see the speedometer but believed the Comet was doing about 100 mph. Traffic was light on Highway 41 and Stump passed the few cars they encountered heading south, red light flashing to warn them. As he cradled Sammy's head, Mark began to pray. Not aloud but silently. At least he tried. Words and thoughts were difficult to form. He remembered Romans 8:26, *"Likewise the Spirit itself also helpeth our infirmities: for we know not what we should pray for as we ought: but the Spirit itself maketh intercession for us with groanings which cannot be uttered."* God, he prayed, you know the situation better than anyone. It's in your hands. Be merciful to this boy and his mother. Twice Stump asked if he was okay and he indicated he was.

He saw the city limit sign for Tadlock, and Stump slowed down--a little. He made a quick left turn on a side street and accelerated for another six blocks and braked to a stop at the emergency room entrance. True to his word, they arrived about fifteen minutes after leaving Gentry.

Someone must have notified the hospital. The doctor and two nurses were waiting at the door with a gurney. Quickly and efficiently, they lifted Sammy's limp body, placed it on the gurney and wheeled it inside. This time, there wasn't even a groan. "Waiting room's inside to the right," Stump said. "Go on in. I'll park my car." As Mark entered the light of the hallway, he could see blood on his shirt and pants. His hands were also covered with blood. A weakness swept over him and he collapsed into the nearest chair and closed his eyes. He sat that way until Harris came and took the next chair, reaching for a cigarette. Eyeing Mark, he said,

"Preacher, you might want to go wash your hands. Men's room is at the end of the hall." Nodding, Mark arose and walked down the hallway, his stomach in a knot over the events of the last hour. He washed his hands and tried to wash some of the blood off his clothes without much success.

As he sat back down, Harris said, "I've seen lots of accidents and people hurt. That boy's hurt bad. May not make it." Turning to look at Mark he continued, "Preacher, you may have to do a funeral."

Mark nodded assent but his stomach lurched, and his heart accelerated. Funeral! He had never done a funeral. The sum of his ministerial experience was the two- and one-half months he had been pastor of the Gentry Baptist Church. Prior to that, he had only preached at churches as a fill-in. He had no idea what a funeral entailed.

Puffing on his cigarette, Stump continued. "If Sammy were to die, it would be really hard on Nell Garber. She lost her husband several years ago. Killed in a traffic accident. Raised Sammy by herself. Losing the boy would be really hard."

In a voice that didn't sound like his own, Mark asked how Mr. Garber died. "He was coming back from Valdosta one day and a log truck couldn't stop at a Stop sign. Brakes failed. Hit his pickup broadside. That was one mangled truck. Didn't think we would ever get his body out." As if remembering it all too well, he inhaled his cigarette and shook his head. "How long ago was it?", Thomas asked. Another puff on the cigarette and Harris replied, "Ten years. He didn't have much life insurance, but Nell got a job in the school cafeteria. She's done a good job raising that boy. He's the light of her life."

Mark heard the doors open and steps in the tiled hallway. Mrs. Garber entered the sitting area accompanied by Harley and Jeanette Bass. Harley was one of the deacons at Gentry Baptist Church. Mrs. Garber was pale, and her eyes were frantic. Both men stood as she stopped and looked at their faces, trying to discern the situation. Mark's tongue stuck to the roof of his mouth. He could say nothing. In a calm voice, Harris said, "Dr. Mixson is with him now. That's all we know." She began to shake and started to faint. They grabbed her and eased her into a chair. Jeanette Bass ran to find a towel and some cold water.

Mrs. Garber opened her eyes, and for the first time noticed the blood on Mark's clothes. She let out a sobbing wail and went limp again. Jeannette Bass came back with a hospital towel and a basin of water. She wet the towel and gently washed the other woman's face all the while speaking words of comfort.

Harley Bass looked at Mark and said, "Preacher, why

don't you lead us in a prayer?" Mark silently chided himself. *Why didn't I think of that? Fine preacher I am!* As they bowed their heads, the door to the emergency room opened and the doctor came out. As he walked toward Mrs. Garber, she hesitantly stood and said, "Dr. Mixson..." and her voice trailed off. The doctor stepped forward, took her hands in his and said, "Mrs. Garber, I'm sorry. There wasn't anything we could do." A look of horror came to her face. Her lips moved as if to say something, but no words would come and then she collapsed. She would have hit the tile floor if the doctor hadn't caught her.

Now it was Mark who thought he would faint or vomit, or something. He had never experienced any emotion like this before--not even when his father died. For the next few minutes, it seemed like a bad dream. Or maybe he was just a spectator but not a part of this tragic scene. He faintly heard the discussion about a sedative for Mrs. Garber, that she should not spend the night alone, Jeanette Bass volunteering to stay with her, and Stump offering to contact Carswell Funeral Home. As the doctor turned to leave, Mrs. Garber roused and asked if she could see the body. Dr. Mixson hesitated and in a pleading voice she said, "Please."

The doctor nodded his assent and said, "Give us a minute to clean him up." She turned to Mark and asked, "Preacher, will you go with me?" Mark nodded. He was getting a crash course in grief ministry. In a few minutes a nurse opened the emergency room door and beckoned for them to enter. Taking her by the arm, Mark walked her across the empty hallway, the sound of their steps on the tile floor echoing off the walls.

The four-bed emergency room was empty except for the figure in the center of the room. Sammy's body was still on the gurney. His clothes had been removed and from the waist down he was covered with a sheet. There was bruising on his torso and the wound on one side of his head was ugly. The nurses had washed off the blood and cleaned him up as best they could. Mark held her tightly as they approached the body.

Mrs. Garber bent over the body and began to gently caress his head, careful not to touch the wound as if it would cause him pain. Almost talking to herself, she said, "He's with Jesus now." As the caressing continued she said, "Preacher, he trusted Jesus as his Savior when he was twelve and has lived as a Christian since then. I know where he is." Mark could remember Sammy always being at church with his mother, active in Sunday School, and serving as an usher on Sunday night, taking up the offering. It occurred to him that he really hadn't had the time to get to know Sammy well. She continued to talk as if Sammy could hear every word. Perhaps ten minutes had passed, and he wondered how long this would last. Just then, she smoothed down his hair, bent over and kissed his cheek, and said, "I'll see you in heaven. Tell Daddy hello for me."

With that, she moved away from the gurney, indicating she was ready to leave. Mark put his arm around her shoulder and could feel her body shudder and she began to sob softly. Crossing the hallway to the waiting room, she turned and thanked him for being there with her. Mark replied, "I'll come by to see you tomorrow." She nodded and said, "I'm ready." She and the Basses left together. Stump excused himself to go and call the funeral home to pick up the body. When he returned, the two men silently crossed the parking lot. The ride home was slower. Nothing was said for several minutes. The farmer/policeman smoked, and the exhausted preacher slumped down in his seat. About halfway home, Stump asked if Sammy had been able to say anything. Mark related the two words the boy had spoken: "Ran" and "Joseph."

"That's all?"

"Yes, I think he tried to say something between those two words, but I couldn't make it out. Like a word connecting those two words."

"Ran *from* Joseph maybe," Stump said. "Is there anyone named Joseph around here" the preacher asked. "No one I've heard of by that name" was the reply. "You're sure that's what he said?"

"Absolutely! Those two words were clear."

"Well that's a puzzle," Stump replied. "Just makes no sense whatsoever. I can't think of anyone he would run from. And I don't know of anyone who would try to hurt the boy."

They approached the city limit sign and the car slowed. It was after midnight and there was no traffic, so Harris pulled across the two southbound lanes and stopped in front of the Cole house. As Mark reached for the door handle, he was stopped by a firm hand gripping his arm. "Preacher, I just want to tell you how much I appreciate what you did tonight. This is going to affect everybody in town. We are all close and a tragedy like this...well, it's just bad for us all." With that he squeezed Mark's arm and let go. With a lump in his throat, Mark nodded a good night and got out.

Crossing the sidewalk, he was surprised to see a light on in the living room. The front door opened, and Edith Cole walked out on the porch. "Preacher are you okay?" she asked.

"Yes ma'am," he replied, "I'm okay." But his mind and heart said otherwise. He knew it would be a while before he would be okay. When she asked about Sammy, he just shook his head.

"Do you want anything to eat or drink?" she asked. "No

ma'am", he replied. "Just need some rest. I'll see you tomorrow."

He went to the back of the house where his apartment entrance was located. Removing the bloody clothes, he took a shower, he got cleaned up and went to bed. The whirring of his window fan drowning out outside noises and usually helped him go to sleep. Tonight was different. Exhausted, both physically and emotionally, he tossed and turned. Would they ever learn *why* Sammy Garber ran out in front of that car? *Who* was he running from? *What* did he mean by "Ran...Joseph?" And *what* would he do for the funeral? The sense of helplessness was overwhelming. He tossed and turned and then he remembered the words of II Corinthians 12:9, *"And he said to me, My grace is sufficient for thee: for my strength is made perfect in weakness. Most gladly therefore will I rather glory in my infirmities, that the power of Christ may rest upon me."*

Staring at the dark ceiling, he prayed for God's strength to empower his weakness and enable him to get through the coming days. After a while, he drifted off into a fitful sleep with dreams of squealing tires, a loud thump, and bloody clothes.

Chapter 2

He awoke at 8:15 and for a moment thought that maybe the events of last night were just a bad dream. Then he saw the blood-stained clothes lying on the floor and knew it was real. What day was it? Friday. He was hungry--really hungry--a hunger that cereal would not satisfy and that was all he kept in the pantry for breakfast. Quickly showering, shaving, and dressing, he walked to the Gentry Restaurant, four blocks away. Gentry had a main intersection if you could call it that. The town's only traffic light was located at the intersection of Highway 41 and County Road 34. On the four corners of the intersection were the restaurant and three service stations. Prior to the building of Interstate 75, the intersection was a busy place, especially during the summer tourist season.

Highway US 41 was the main corridor for tourists

coming to Florida from the central northern states. Now, most of the business was from local people.

At 8:30, the restaurant was deserted, the early morning breakfast crowd already gone to work. As the door closed behind him, he was greeted by the owner, Myrtle Johns. After retiring from the Navy, Clarence and Myrtle Johns had come home to Gentry. They bought the restaurant, which Myrtle ran, and Clarence drove a school bus. He joked that he took the job because driving a bus was easy--it loaded and unloaded itself. Myrtle nodded as he walked in. "You had a tough night, preacher. You need some breakfast?" He ordered the special: two eggs, grits, bacon, and toast with coffee. Taking a seat at a corner table, his mind went to the funeral and what he should say or do. Myrtle brought his food and after a blessing, he quickly devoured the meal. Myrtle was pouring his second cup of coffee when Stump Harris came in.

"Just coffee, Myrtle" as he walked to Mark's table and sat down. "Get any sleep," he asked. "Some," was the reply.

"Well, I didn't get much. I saw a lot of men die in the war, but seeing a young'un die, well, it's harder to take. Just don't seem fair." Myrtle brought his coffee so he took a minute to sip it and smoke.

Stump was not his real name. It was Hoyt Emanuel, but

few people knew that. He was called Stump because of his physique--5'7" and about 210 pounds, a barrel chest, broad shoulders, and big, muscular arms. In high school he had been an exceptionally good football player, joking that he played the right side of the line. For a person of his size, he was quick and surprisingly agile and might have played college football if not for the war. Graduating from Gentry High School in 1942, he immediately volunteered for the Army. He was in the invasion of Italy and fought in some of the worst battles of WW II. His courage and leadership quickly advanced him to the rank of Sergeant. More than one GI owed his life to Stump's courage, not to mention his marksmanship. After his discharge, he returned to Gentry to marry his high school sweetheart, Alma, and take over the family farm.

He and Alma had planned on several kids, but the years passed, and none were born. Alma taught second grade at the elementary school and lavished her love on the students who passed through her class. Stump was an avid supporter of the Gentry sports teams, often discreetly providing money to help a boy pay for needed equipment.

A chain smoker, he pulled out a fresh cigarette and lit it off the stub of the one he just finished. The joke was that whatever he spent on cigarettes, he saved on matches. Taking another sip of coffee, he said, "Let's talk about last night. Been thinking about some of the details. Did you say Sammy ran out from that dirt road between Edith's and 241?"

"Yes, is that important?"

Another sip of coffee and another puff of cigarette. "Maybe, maybe not. What was he doing over there? The only explanation that makes sense is, that's where his girlfriend lives." This was new information for Mark. He wasn't aware that Sammy had a girlfriend, but then, he'd only known the boy for a couple of months. It's just that he hadn't seen Sammy with a girl, at least not at church.

Myrtle came with the coffee pot and refilled their cups. Stump continued. "Her name is Sue Kelly. They live on past the curve in that road going down behind the school. I'm thinking we need to have a talk with her. See if he was over at her house and maybe why he was running."

Mark contemplated that for a minute and asked, "Would it be appropriate? I mean, this quick after he died. I'm sure she must be upset too."

"Oh no," was the reply. "Not today. Maybe some time next week. I'll see when we can go over and talk with her. Besides, I've got to take a load of hogs to the sale today."

"Stump, you said we. What do you mean 'we'?"

Through the haze of smoke that he was generating Stump replied, "You are as close as I have to a witness to what happened. I would appreciate it if you would go with me when I talk to her."

"What about the driver of the car?"

"Don't think he'd be much help," said Stump. "Anyway, he's gone home to Ocala. Sheriff's deputy and Highway Patrol investigated the accident scene and took his statement. Everything backs up his and your story of what happened. I looked this morning. Skid marks show where he tried to stop."

"Who was he? And why was he driving through Gentry if he lived in Ocala?"

"A traveling salesman. He was planning on spending the night in Tadlock. Going to call on a customer there today. Sheriff's office knows how to contact him if we need him." Standing up he took fifty cents out of his pocket and laid it on the table. "I'll see about us talking to the Kelly's. Maybe they can shed some light on 'ran…Joseph'. See you later."

Myrtle came with the coffee pot, but he declined. "How many funerals have you done?", she asked. He exhaled a sigh and replied, "This is my first one. This is my first church." She patted him on the shoulder and said, "You'll do okay." I wish I were as confident, he thought. As he reached for his wallet, she said, "This one's on the house preacher." When Mark asked why, she made a pretense of being offended and replied, "Because I want to, that's why." Then her face softened into a smile and she went on. "Preacher, you are a part of this town now and we appreciate you." A part of this town! He had never felt that form of acceptance before. At times in his life, he had felt he was part of his family, or a class or his team, or his Air Force group, but had never been told he was part of a town. He nodded a response and started back home. It was almost ten o'clock and the August heat and humidity made him perspire.

He took his Bible, a commentary on the Gospel of Matthew, and a Blue Horse composition book and sat at the small dining table. The church did not have a pastor's office, so he studied at home. His library, such as it was, filled a four-shelf bookcase. A retired pastor had given him a complete set of Barnes Notes. His church in Valdosta had allowed him to take extra copies of January Bible Study books that had accumulated over the years; and he had bought a concordance and Bible dictionary. If he fulfilled his goal of attending seminary, he knew his book collection would grow.

Before he started studying, he prayed and asked for wisdom as he completed his Sunday night sermon, a series on The Lord's Prayer. As he prayed, his thoughts went to

Mrs. Garber and he began praying for her. "Lord, give her the strength she needs for these days. Show your love to her, may she feel your presence." He prayed that the funeral would be a testimony to Sammy's faith and help the small community deal with the grief of his death.

With his Bible open to Matthew 6 and the commentary, he read and made notes for his sermon. Mark was grateful for a suggestion his pastor in Valdosta had made. After expressing his lack of training in sermon study and preparation, his pastor suggested, "There are several Baptist churches in Valdosta. Why don't you visit them and listen to the different sermon presentations? Take notes. We did this in seminary, and it was most helpful." So for months, he rotated from church to church, listening and learning.

The section of the Lord's Prayer for this week's sermon was in verse 10: *"Thy will be done in earth, as it is in heaven."* He began listing statements that would be the main points of the sermon.

-How can we know God's will for our lives?

-The challenge of following God's will.

-Are we following God's will for our lives?

He then added one more statement: Am I following God's will for my life? He underlined the "I", laid down his pen and reflected about how God's will had brought him to Gentry, Florida.

~

Mark Thomas spent the first eighteen years of his life on a small farm near Bishop, Georgia, just south of Athens. An only child, he was generously loved but not spoiled. His parents believed in hard work, responsibility, truthfulness, and courtesy. Upon graduation from high school, he enlisted in the Air Force for two reasons: a chance to travel and see the world and qualify to for the GI bill to attend college. His dream of seeing some of the world never materialized. Every assignment was in the United States, his last year at Moody AFB in Valdosta, Georgia.

It was a foregone conclusion that he would return home and attend the University of Georgia, but a sequence of events changed that plan. The first was the death of his father from a heart attack while he was stationed at Moody AFB. Then his mother sold the farm and moved to Athens to live with her sister Catherine, also a widow. During his year at Moody, he developed a liking for Valdosta, home to Valdosta State College. The small college campus appealed to him and he decided to attend VSC. A part-time job at the Belk-Hudson store helped with expenses.

During his junior year in college, he surrendered to the ministry and focused on preparing himself to be a preacher. Nearing graduation in the spring of 1964, he was undecided about his future. He could enroll in seminary in the fall but couldn't decide which one to attend. The closest ones were in Louisville, Kentucky and New Orleans, Louisiana. A second option was to seek to pastor a church, if any church would be interested in someone as inexperienced as he was. A third option was to work full-time for a year at Belk-Hudson, pay off some bills and save some money for seminary.

He often discussed his future with the director of the Baptist Student Union at the college and requested the prayers of fellow students during Bible study sessions. Just before graduation, the BSU director summoned him and shared that the Baptist church in Gentry, Florida was looking for a pastor. It was a small church but could afford a pastor who didn't have a family to support. He suggested Mark pray about it and a week later, he felt he should pursue the opportunity. After meeting with the deacons who functioned as a pastor search committee, he preached on the last Sunday of May and the congregation voted to call him as pastor.

So here he was. Twenty-five years old, a college graduate, single, pastoring his first church, and still very unsure of what he was doing. But...he was certain beyond a shadow of a doubt that God had brought him to Gentry. Bowing his head, he thanked God for the divine guidance in his life, for directing his life to Gentry, and asking for guidance to be the pastor he needed to be. Picking up the Parker pen his Aunt Nell had given him for graduation, he continued to make notes for the sermon.

The front door of the house opened and closed, signaling that Mrs. Cole was home for lunch. He went out and around the house to ask to use the phone to call Mrs. Garber and see about a convenient time to talk about the funeral. There was no phone in the apartment, but Mrs. Cole allowed him to use hers. Telling her his purpose, she said, "938-4325." In addition to knowing such details as who was related to whom, people's occupations, and other details, she also seemed to know everyone's phone number.

He dialed the number and Jeanette Bass answered on the second ring. He was glad to know she was with the bereaved woman. "Mrs. Bass, this is Mark Thomas. I was calling to see when a convenient time would be to see Mrs. Garber." She said to hold a minute and he heard her relay the question. "How about three o'clock preacher?" He responded that would be good. Thanking Mrs. Cole for the use of the phone, he returned to his part of the house and made a pimento cheese sandwich for lunch. Afterwards, he continued to work on the sermon.

Chapter 3

At 2:45, he picked up his Bible and a Blue Horse composition book. He had used these inexpensive composition books since high school, and they were convenient for making study notes. He crossed Highway 41 and walked east to the railroad tracks, crossed over and walked two more blocks to the Garber house. It was a small, two-bedroom frame house sitting in a well-kept yard. Jeanette Bass answered his knock on the screen door, invited him in and led him to the dining room where Nell Garber was seated.

He was amazed at the difference in her appearance from last night. Her eyes were red, and she twisted a white handkerchief embroidered in lavender with her hands. But there was a resolve on her face that was surprising. Her Bible and a sheet of notebook paper with some notes lay on the table. "Have a seat Preacher," she said in a soft voice.

"Mrs. Garber, before we go any further, there's something I feel you deserve to know." Her eyebrows arched inquisitively. He continued. "You know this is my first church?" She nodded that she did. "Well, I have never done a funeral service before. Perhaps you would want to consider someone with more experience than me. Maybe one of your former pastors. Someone who could say the right words. If you decided to do that, I wouldn't be offended. I would understand completely."

She took a moment to respond and Mark thought perhaps she could see the benefit of his suggestion. Then she spoke. "Preacher, lots of folks can say good words but don't have the feelings to go with their words. You have the feelings. You proved that last night by what you did for Sammy. I will never forget what you did for him." He dropped his head as his eyes watered up. "Thank you," he said, "I appreciate that."

"Not as much as I do", she replied. "No, Preacher, there is no one else I want to do the funeral. And besides, you're our preacher." There was an emphasis on the "our preacher". Looking back up, he said, "Well, let's begin with prayer."

The three bowed their heads and Mark began to pray. "Lord, there are some things in life we just don't understand. They don't make sense to us. We just don't see things as you see them. But we believe what Paul said in Romans 8 that all things work together for good for those of us who love you and you love us. What we don't understand now, we will understand completely one day, and it will make perfect sense to us. As that great old hymn says, 'We will understand it better by and by.' Now I pray you would give Mrs. Garber an extra measure of your mercy, love, and grace during these difficult days. Wrap your loving arms around her and hold her close. Guide us as we plan the service for Sammy, who is now in your presence. Amen."

While he was praying, he wondered where his words were coming from? Where did those thoughts come from? After the "Amen" Mrs. Garber reached across the table and squeezed his hand. "Thank you, Preacher. That was a beautiful prayer. I needed that." Jeanette Bass was sniffing and wiping her nose with a tissue.

She picked up the piece of notebook paper and said, "I've made the arrangements with Carswell's. The service will be at the church Monday morning at ten. That way, it won't be as hot, and we won't have to worry about the afternoon showers." Mark made a note in his composition book and then asked, "Is the viewing on Sunday night?" It was customary to have the viewing the night before the service. "No," she replied, shaking her head. "The viewing will be from 3:00 to 5:00 on Sunday afternoon. That way, folks don't have to miss church. Folk's need to be in church on

Sunday night." Mark had another sense of appreciation for this dear woman. In the midst of her personal sorrow and grief, she was considerate of others.

Returning to her notes, she continued. "I would like for you to use John 14:1-6 as your scripture. That to me is a special promise that Jesus made to us."

"I would be glad to use it."

"Now, for the pallbearers, I am asking the boys who were on the basketball team with him." Mark would later learn that Sammy was a good basketball player and one of the leading scorers on last year's team. "And Gail Smith will sing two songs: *Amazing Grace* and *It Is Well with My Soul*. She has a beautiful voice." Mark nodded in agreement. Gail Smith did have a beautiful voice and was asked to sing for many funerals. Since he had never conducted a funeral, Mark was flying by the seat of his pants. Before coming over, he had tried to remember what was done at the funerals he had attended. It's funny how you can attend something and observe what takes place but can't remember it. As he looked at the notes he had made, it occurred to him to think about an order of the service. When would Gail sing? At what point would he do the sermon? He asked Mrs. Garber if she had any preference? She didn't; so he suggested a hymn, the greeting, obituary, and a prayer, another hymn, and the message. She thought about it for a moment and nodded her assent. She then asked, "Preacher, what about the graveside? Are you going to do another whole sermon like some preachers do?" Jeanette Bass stifled a laugh. "To be honest, I hadn't thought about the graveside, but no, I don't see the need to preach another sermon as you put it. I would say, read a passage of scripture, such as Psalm 23 and pray."

"I like that," she said. "I won't call names, but we have a few preachers who preach a whole 'nother sermon at the grave." He smiled and said, "I promise you I won't do that. Is there anything else we need to cover?" Mrs. Garber squirmed a little and then asked, as if she were ashamed to bring it up, "What do you charge for doing a funeral?" The question was unexpected, and Mark stammered for an answer. "Why, nothing. This is part of my duty as your pastor." She exchanged a quick glance with Jeanette Bass who gave a nod of approval. "Well then, I guess we have it done."

As he pushed his chair away from the table, Jeanette said, "I'm fixing to put on a pot of coffee, and we were going to have a piece of cake. Won't you stay and join us?" He was about to reply in the negative when he spotted the big coconut cake sitting on the counter in the kitchen. "Why, thank you. I believe I will."

For the next half hour, he and the two women ate cake, drank coffee, and made small talk, avoiding any comments about Sammy's death. Both women asked him questions about his family. Nell Garber occasionally wiped her tears but seemed to shed some of the strain and tension that gripped her. He was tempted to ask her if she knew what "ran...Joseph" might mean but his better judgement told him there would be a more appropriate time. When he said his goodbyes and left, he walked home feeling he had bonded with the two women in a significant way. In the days to come, he would find out just how strong that bond was.

Chapter 4

On Saturday, he awoke just before 7:00 AM. As he rolled out of bed he thought, this is more like it. Almost back to his normal wake-up of 6:00 AM. There was no reason for him to awake so early and he didn't even set the alarm. His years in the Air Force had conditioned him to get up at 6:00 each morning and he couldn't break the habit.

As he showered, he had a desire for breakfast at the restaurant. Shaving and dressing, he was closing the door when, on impulse, he picked up his Bible and a composition book.

When he opened the door of the restaurant, Myrtle greeted him with, "You again? This is getting to be habit." Mark jokingly replied, "It's the outstanding quality of the food that brings me back."

"Flattery won't get you a free meal today," she retorted in good humor. "You've got to pay for this one. Us Methodists are generous, but only up to a point." They laughed and she asked what he wanted. "The special, I guess."

"Do you like buttermilk pancakes?" she asked. Did he like them! He loved them! It was his favorite breakfast growing up and he hadn't had any good ones since he left home.

"Buttermilk pancakes and bacon." Myrtle brought coffee and then headed to the kitchen. In a few minutes she returned with a plate stacked so high with pancakes that she had to put the bacon on another plate. He said a silent blessing and began to eat with gusto. The pancakes were maybe the best he had ever eaten. As she watched him eat, she said, "Preacher, what you need is a wife to cook you good meals every day." Between bites he replied, "Not much chance of that happening." With a sly smile she said, "Oh, you never know."

After she made the rounds with the coffee pot, she returned to his table as he finished the last of the pancakes. "Myrtle, those are the best I've ever eaten, but don't tell my Mama, she would write me out of her will." As she removed the empty plate, he asked if it would be okay if he used the table to do some studying. "Sure", she replied. He explained that he needed to make some notes for the funeral sermon.

Just then he had a thought. "Myrtle tell me about Sammy Garber. What kind of person was he?"

With a, "Just a minute," she took the dirty plates to the kitchen and came back and sat down. "He was a really good kid and I mean good. Probably the politest kid in Gentry. And he was a good worker. Worked for Pete Sims in the store since he was fifteen. Saved his money too. Most boys save their money to buy a car. Sammy saved his to go to college. He wanted to be a sportswriter for a newspaper. That boy was a walking authority on sports. You name it--football, basketball, baseball. College or professional. He could tell you the scores of every big-league baseball game played yesterday and details about who pitched and who got hits and homeruns. He planned to go to the two-year college in Madison and then maybe to the University of Florida. Said they had a good school of journalism. Read the sports section of the Florida Times Union and the Valdosta Daily Times every day."

He was busy making notes and she paused as if he needed to catch up. When he stopped writing, she continued. "And he was a good Christian. I mean, for him, it was more than just a Sunday thing. He lived what he learned out of the Bible. And do you know he was always helping people? Yes. Anyone he saw who needed help, he would offer, especially older folks and widows. Oh, Lord, the widows of this town loved him. You know preacher, his life may have been short, but it was well lived."

Suddenly the light went off in his head. What was that Mrs. Garber had said about John 14:1-6? The most special promise that Jesus made. A life that was lived and a promise fulfilled. Sammy's life and John 14:1-6. That was his funeral sermon! As Myrtle excused herself to wait on a customer, he began to write additional notes. He opened his Bible to John 14 and for the next half-hour the pen seemed to flow across the lines of its own accord. It was almost 9:00 when he put the cap on his pen and closed the composition book. He left money on the table for his meal and tip. Telling Myrtle thanks, he headed home.

By the time he reached the house he was restless and had an urge to go somewhere, to get out of Gentry for a little while. He considered driving down to Matlock but decided against it since he didn't know anyone there. That left Valdosta--little bit farther to drive, but it was familiar. As he walked to his car, a Ford Falcon, he realized that the car hadn't been driven in days. One of the benefits of a small town was that he could walk anywhere in ten minutes, so the car wasn't necessary unless it was raining. Pulling out on Highway 41, he headed for Valdosta, avoiding I-75. A leisurely drive took him through Lake Park, Twin Lakes, and Dasher. The car was not air conditioned which necessitated rolling down the windows to allow the outside air to blow through. As he drove, he could feel the tension subside in his body and realized just how much stress the last two days had brought.

Upon reaching the downtown area of Valdosta, he wondered where he would go and what he would do. Parking on Patterson Street, he got out and walked around, looking in store windows. He stopped in Belk-Hudson and chatted with some former co-workers and then went to Woolworth's for a soda. Sitting at the counter he felt a pang of loneliness in a way he hadn't experienced before. There had been times of loneliness when he was in the Air Force, stationed in a strange place where he knew no one. But this was something new and different. Something he couldn't describe. And he didn't like it.

He left Woolworth's and browsed up Patterson Street and then cut over to Ashley and worked his way back to his car. Getting in, he just sat for a few minutes, contemplating where to go next. The feeling of loneliness was still there. Maybe Myrtle was right. Maybe he did need a wife. What was he thinking! He wasn't even dating anyone!

He had dated a few girls while in the Air Force and even more at Valdosta State. The dating was mostly among friends for companionship, to go to a movie or skiing in Twin Lakes. He was never serious about any of the girls he dated, remembering some advice his father gave him. "Son," he said, "don't get serious about a girl unless she's a Christian and she's the one you want to spend the rest of your life with." That was the extent of the dating advice his father gave him, but he saw the love his parents had for each other and knew that's what he wanted when he did marry.

The issue of his being single was one of the things the deacons in Gentry had discussed with him. It was a concern to some that he was twenty-five and not married. He could have given answers such as he didn't want to get serious with anyone while in the military and unsure of where he may be transferred and while in college, he was more focused on getting his education than getting married. What he did tell them was that God just hadn't brought the right person into his life yet. That answer satisfied even the most skeptical deacons. Maybe that's it, he thought. God just hasn't brought her into my life yet.

Cranking the car, he drove north on Patterson, past the campus, and then thought of Shoney's and strawberry pie. Cutting over to Ashley Street, he pulled into a crowded parking lot. Entering, he was surprised to see Gail Smith sitting alone in a booth. She saw him and motioned for him to come over. They spoke and she asked if he was shopping. He told her no, just needed to get away for a little while. "Me too," she replied. "I say I'm coming to shop yet buy little.

Looking down at the table she added, "But always strawberry pie."

"That's what brought me here," he said. With a doubtful look she said, "You drove all the way to Valdosta just for strawberry pie?" They both laughed and he realized it was the first time he had really laughed in weeks.

"Won't you join me?", she asked.

He quickly replied, "I don't want to be a bother."

She smiled and replied, "It's no bother. I'm alone and some conversation would be nice." He accepted and slid in the booth opposite her. He ordered a Big Boy and coke and a slice of strawberry pie. Waiting on his food, he reflected on the first time he ever saw Gail Smith.

~

It was the Saturday before Christmas last year. He was working the evening schedule in the men's department at Belk-Hudson. Shoppers had made havoc of the men's shirt counter and he was straightening and putting the sizes in their correct space. He was lost in thought about driving to Athens the following day to spend Christmas with his mother and Aunt Catherine. The department manager had given him some days off so he could have four days for Christmas, even though it meant driving back on Christmas day to work on the 26th. He was not aware that anyone was in the department when he heard a woman's voice ask, "Excuse me. Could you help me please?" He looked up into a face that caused him to momentarily lose his composure. It was not a beautiful face when compared with some young women, but it was a wholesome, attractive face with black hair and green eyes. She was petite, maybe 5'3".

Regaining his composure, he said, "I'm sorry. How may I help you?" She held up a tie and a package of handkerchiefs. "I would like to purchase these items." He took them and led her to the cash register where she paid, and he bagged the items. She then asked if she could get the items gift wrapped and he directed her to the second floor. Thanking him, she walked toward the elevator and left him wondering who she was and where did she live and was she married. The answer to the last question was possibly yes, since she had purchased gifts for a man. Anyway, chances were slim he would ever see her again. He sighed and returned to straightening the shirt counter.

The Sunday he went to preach in view of a call at Gentry Baptist Church, she was there! When they were introduced, she smiled and said, "I think we've met. You sold me a tie and some handkerchiefs." As if she could read his mind, she said with a hint of a smile, "They were for my brother and our school principal. I teach English at the high school." Stealing a glance at her left hand, he didn't see a ring, so evidently she wasn't married. After becoming the pastor of Gentry Baptist Church, he saw a great deal of her. She sang in the choir and she and her mother rarely missed attending church. Gail was the church secretary/clerk, a volunteer position. She kept membership records, ordered literature, and handled correspondence and bills for the church. She was always cordial and friendly, but she was that way with everyone.

"I'm not sure if this is a late lunch or early supper," he said.

"I'm sure these last two days have been difficult," she said. "I understand this is your first funeral." For the next few minutes they talked about Sammy's tragic death.

"Mrs. Garber says you're going to sing at the funeral," he said.

"Yes, and it won't be easy. I have known Sammy all his life and he was one of my students, one of my better students." Her eyes began to water. As he was wondering how to respond, the waitress brought his meal and he was grateful for the distraction. She bowed her head as he asked the blessing and resumed eating her pie as he ate. As he put the fork on the empty pie plate, he remarked, "I was hungrier than I thought." He was wondering how to resume the conversation when she said, "I'm curious, what brought you to Gentry?"

With a wry smile, he replied, "That's a story in itself."

Propping her elbows on the table, she said, "I'd like to hear it." So he told her about his life, his call to the ministry, and the events that led to him going to Gentry. He finished with, "That's the abbreviated version of the life of Mark Thomas." Taking a sip of his coke, he said, "Now, tell me your story."

"It's really short and simple. I grew up in Gentry, graduated, and went to Florida State University. I had planned to stay in Tallahassee and teach. My older brother and his family live there. But the summer I graduated, Dad had a stroke that left him partially paralyzed, so I moved back to help mother take care of him. Gentry High had an opening for an English teacher, so I took the job and have taught for two years. Mark quickly did the math: Eighteen when she graduated, four years in college, and two years teaching. That means she was about twenty-four. One year younger than he was. "And your father?"

"He died last year. Mom doesn't really need me now, but I don't have any desire to move away." There was a silent pause and then she asked a question that surprised him.

"How long do you think you will be in Gentry?"

"Well..." he paused. Why did she ask? How should he answer? "I'm really not sure. I would like to go to seminary at some point. I feel I need that level of education to be a more effective preacher and pastor."

"And where would that be?"

"Probably New Orleans or Louisville." She looked out the plate glass window as if envisioning something and said, "It might be nice to live in a large city like that." One topic led to another and they talked and even laughed a couple of times. In the process they discovered that they had several mutual interests. She told him how much she enjoyed his sermons. He was gratified by her compliment and at the same time, felt a little self-conscious. "You make it easy to understand and I think that's something our members appreciate."

When she finally said she needed to go, he looked at his watch and was surprised to see that two hours had passed. It seemed like just a few minutes. He took both tickets and over her protest said, "Let me. It's been a long time since I've treated anyone." As they left the restaurant, he walked her to her car, a Nash Metropolitan, turquoise and white, with only two seats. He remarked that it was a nifty car.

"It was my college graduation present from Mother and Daddy." He opened the door for her and said, "Perhaps we can do this again sometime."

She smiled and replied, "Maybe. See you tomorrow." It took a second to register. Tomorrow, yes, tomorrow is Sunday, I will see her tomorrow. Mark stood watching as she exited the parking lot. I could enjoy more of her company, he said to himself. He was in a much better mood as he drove back to Gentry.

Chapter 5

On the morning of the funeral, Mark set his alarm for
7:00am, not wanting to risk any chance of oversleeping. He
was to unlock the church at 8:00 for Henry Carswell. Time
enough to eat breakfast. After starting the coffee, he poured a
bowl of cereal and reached for a banana, but the fruit bowl
was empty. Got to go to Tuttle's. Gentry had three small
grocery stores. They didn't carry the selection of the IGA in
Tadlock, but he didn't buy a lot of groceries, mostly
something for breakfast and lunch. He bought at Tuttle's
because they were members of his church. Bob was a deacon
and Miriam taught Sunday School. He emptied the carton of
milk on the cereal. He had to go to Tuttle's--today.

The first couple of weeks he lived in Mrs. Cole's
apartment he cooked, or attempted to cook, his supper. One
day at lunch, she knocked on his screen and asked if he

would join her for supper--fried pork chops, fresh vegetables, and cornbread. He accepted the invitation without hesitation. After the meal that night she said, "Why don't you just plan on eating supper with me?" He said, "You mean, every night?"

"Yes, that's what I mean."

"But Mrs. Cole, I don't want to put you to all that trouble," he protested. "It's no trouble at all," she replied. "Cooking for two is just as easy as cooking for one."

He considered her most gracious offer and then, "Okay, if you'll let me buy some of the groceries."

In a very affirmative voice, she replied, "No! It's something I want to do." As he tried to think of a reasonable reply, her tone softened and she said, "Eating alone is no fun. I've done it for five years now. It will be worth the cost of the groceries just to have company." With a sly smile she added, "Besides, this keeps me from having to eat leftovers."

"Are you absolutely sure?" he asked. "I'm sure," was her reply.

Since that time, he only bought food for breakfast and lunch and happily enjoyed Mrs. Cole's cooking for supper.

Finishing his cereal, he washed the bowl and spoon, poured a cup of coffee, and moved to one of the easy chairs.

Taking his Bible and the notes he had made for the funeral, he read over them, changing a couple of words for something that was more appropriate for what he was trying to say.

At 8:00, he slipped on a sport shirt and khakis and went to unlock the church. The AC had been left on last night, so the building was comfortable. He hoped it would stay that way. Returning to the house, he drank another cup of coffee and thought about what lay ahead. Bowing his head, he prayed for everyone involved in the funeral-himself, Gail, Maude Hogan, who was the church pianist, and any others. Lastly, he prayed for Nell Garber. In the space of a few years, she had lost the two loves of her life--her husband and son. Mark couldn't even begin to imagine the depth of her grief and sorrow. He concluded his prayer by asking that the service be a testimony to Sammy Garber and his faith in Jesus Christ.

He purposely waited to take a shower and get dressed. The August heat and humidity would be terrible today. Not a good day to have to wear a suit and tie, especially outside. At 8:30, he showered, shaved, and opened the closet. He owned two suits--one blue, one gray--with matching ties, and four white dress shirts. He really needed to buy another suit. His mother and Aunt Catherine had each sent him money for his birthday last month and he would use it to buy another suit. Taking out the blue one, he dressed and headed for the church.

Henry Carswell and two assistants were there. The casket was situated in front of the communion table and they were busy placing flower arrangements around it and the platform. When he entered, Henry came over and shook his hand. "Going to be a hot one preacher. Glad we are doing it this morning." Mark nodded in agreement. The funeral director said, "You know the routine?" Unsure of what he meant, Mark replied, "No."

"You know, how our part and your part work together."

"Mr. Carswell, this is my first funeral service. I must confess, I don't know about the routine as you call it." Henry Carswell stared at him for a moment as if he thought Mark might be joking. Realizing Mark was being truthful, he said, "Okay, let me explain. We will seat the people as they come in. If you want, you can mingle and speak to folks. That's up to you. The casket will be open so folks can view the body. We will close it just before we bring Mrs. Garber in. You can go ahead and sit on the platform or meet us outside and walk in with us, your choice. After we seat Mrs. Garber, I will motion for the congregation to be seated and that's when your part of the service will begin--the singing and preaching." He paused as if to see if Mark understood. Nodding that he did, Henry continued. "Preacher, how will you end the service? In other words, what's the last thing you will do?"

"I will conclude with a prayer." Henry nodded. "Okay, when you finish praying, step down by the side of the casket. We will come down and take over from there. Oh, one more thing. How about the graveside?"

"It will be brief. I will read the 23rd Psalm and pray." The funeral director had a look of unbelief. "That's it? No more preaching?" When Mark assured him that would be the duration of the graveside service, Henry's face took on a look of relief and he nodded his agreement. "That'll be good preacher, that'll be good."

The funeral wasn't until 10:00 but people started arriving about 9:15. Many of those who went down to view Sammy's body walked away crying. By 9:40, the church was almost full, and Henry Carswell went down forward and asked that people bunch up in order to create more room. People were even seated in the choir loft. Mark suspected that many of the mourners would not be able to get a seat in the church. What a day to have to stand outside, he thought. At least there were some shady oaks on the north side of the church.

At 9:45, Carswell told him he was going to pick up Mrs. Garber. The round trip of six blocks wouldn't take long.

Mark proceeded to move to his chair on the platform. There were two large, padded pulpit chairs, one on either side of the pulpit. He tried to get Gail to use one, but she preferred to sit in a chair next to the piano. At 9:55, the two assistants came down and closed the casket.

When the black Cadillac stopped in front of the church and Henry Carswell helped Nell Garber out, Mark had a sudden change of mind. He quickly stepped off the platform and walked out to where they were standing. An expression of relief crossed Nell's face. Without speaking he took her hand and she squeezed it as if to thank him.

One of the assistants asked the congregation to rise and then the other assistant seated the pallbearers. The pallbearers, Sammy's teammates, wore dark pants, white dress shirts and clip-on ties. After they were seated, Henry Carswell escorted Mrs. Garber and Mark to the front right pew. Mark released her hand and returned to his seat on the platform and the funeral director motioned for the congregation to sit.

Gail waited for a few seconds before she stood to sing. The church did not have a sound system but really didn't need one. The acoustics were particularly good, and her voice carried out over the congregation. As they heard the words of *Amazing Grace*, many began to cry softly. It was mostly the women and girls who cried. The men sat with stoic faces, masking the emotions they felt. Mark glanced at the pallbearers, the basketball team. It was unusual to see teenage boys crying. They did not sob as the girls did, but their eyes were red, and they continually wiped the tears off their cheeks.

It was a new experience for them, Mark thought. Teenagers don't think about dying. In their way of thinking, only old people died. He knew because there was a time when he thought that way too.

As he scanned the crowded church, the thought ran through his mind that possibly someone here may know why Sammy Garber ran out in front of that car. Possibly someone who knew *why* he was running and *what* he was running from. His eyes caught the eyes of Stump Harris and he knew the part-time lawman was thinking the same thing. It was almost amusing to see the man in a suit and tie. He appeared to be choking, constantly tugging on the collar of the starched white shirt. As he scanned the crowd one more time, it seemed that one person wasn't displaying grief in the normal way, and it was Mrs. Kelly. Mark had met the Kelly family at the viewing the previous afternoon. The first thing he noticed was that Mrs. Kelly was several years younger than Mr. Kelly and he learned that she was Sue's stepmother. Mrs. Kelly had an expression on her face that indicated she would rather be anywhere than where she was. She was fidgety and seemed uncomfortable. Oh well, he thought, not everyone deals with grief the same way.

Gail finished her song and he stood and approached the pulpit. After thanking everyone for their care and concern for Mrs. Garber, he said the service was a celebration of Sammy Garber's life. The apostle Paul wrote that to be absent from the body was to be present with the Lord. He illustrated that by saying that when a student was absent from school, they were present somewhere else. Sammy was absent from them, but he was in the presence of the Lord. He encouraged them to remember that. After reading the obituary information, he prayed and sat down.

Gail stood, and Maude began to play *It Is Well with My Soul*. This time, Mark did not scan the congregation. Instead, he turned to look at Gail as she sang. She was facing the congregation and could not see him. As he looked at her profile and heard her beautiful voice, he remembered the two hours they had spent at Shoney's Saturday night. For a moment, his mind drifted and then he heard the words of the chorus: *It is well with my soul, it is well, it is well with my soul*. Mark knew that would be appropriate for his sermon.

When she finished and was seated, he took a deep breath and said to himself, here goes. Placing his Bible and notes on the pulpit he began. "I said that we are here to celebrate the life of Sammy Garber. I have two points to make in my sermon: One, a life lived; and two, a promise fulfilled. I must confess that I didn't have the opportunity to get to know Sammy very well and from all I've heard, that's my misfortune. But from what some of you have told me, Sammy lived his life in a good, positive, wholesome, Christian way. I don't think anyone here has regrets as a result of Sammy's life being a failure. His life was anything but a failure. He did his best in everything. He wasn't perfect, none of us are. But he lived life to the fullest."

He paused and saw heads nodding in agreement. "I'm going to ask you to do something that may be strange, especially for a funeral service; but please, help me. If Sammy ever encouraged you, raise your hand." Many students raised their hands, including all the pallbearers, his basketball teammates. "You may put them down. Now, if Sammy ever did something to help you out, raise your hand." Hands of all ages went up, noticeably the widows. "Thank you. You may put them down. Now, if Sammy ever shared his faith in Jesus with you, raise your hand." This time the response was slower, almost reluctant, but several students raised their hands. "Now, if you raised your hand for any of these three things, raise it again." All over the church, hands went up. "Hold them there, keep them up. Folks, look around." Mark estimated that sixty to seventy percent of those in the congregation had their hands raised. "Here is proof that Sammy had an impact on your life. Your life is better in some way because you knew him." Smiles and nods were apparent on many faces. He went on to talk about the special qualities that made Sammy the person and friend that he had been. He reminded them that Sammy had experienced hardship when he lost his father but didn't allow that to change him or warp his life.

Then he moved on to his second point: A promise fulfilled. He read John 14:1-6 and then elaborated. "Jesus has made a promise to every believer, that when our earthly life is ended, he will take us to that eternal, heavenly home he is currently preparing for us. Our great loss has been Sammy's gain. He is in a better place, living a better life than anything we can imagine." Mark avoided being critical or condemning, but he challenged everyone to trust Jesus as their Savior while they had the opportunity. "A week ago, who of us knew we would be here today, saying goodbye to Sammy? The Bible says that our lives are like a vapor or mist. We are so fragile, our life is limited, and none of us know when it may come to an end. Think about the words of the song Miss Smith sang. Is it well with your soul?"

He concluded, closed his Bible, and requested the congregation bow for prayer. As per instructions, when he finished praying, he stepped down beside the casket. Thankfully, Mrs. Garber did not want it opened again so the time in the church would not be extended. As Henry Carswell motioned for people to stand, soft sobbing resumed, especially among the teenage girls.

Carswell had told Mark he could ride in the Cadillac to the cemetery, some two miles out of town. When Henry opened the front passenger side door for her, she shook her head and got in the back seat with Mark. She reached for his hand and whispered, "Thank you. It was perfect." The lump in his throat wouldn't allow him to speak so he returned her squeeze.

The graveside was as brief as Mark promised. He read the 23rd Psalm and prayed. He stepped to one side and allowed Carswell to say that the service was concluded that the church had provided a meal for out of town family members and friends, and that the grave site would be ready for viewing in the afternoon. He then assisted Nell Garber to her feet and led her to the shade of a massive oak tree where mourners moved to speak to her. This was Mark's first trip to the Gentry cemetery and as he looked around, he wondered how many more trips he might make. Several people came by and complimented him on the service.

Henry Carswell came over and asked if he was ready to return to the church. Mark nodded and they returned to the Cadillac. Harley and Jeanette Bass had offered to drive Nell Garber back to the church. Henry turned the AC on high and it felt good. Pulling back on the highway he said, "Are you sure this was your first funeral?" When Mark replied that it was, he grunted and said, "Sure couldn't tell it."

Several of the ladies of the church were finishing preparations for the meal for Nell Garber's out of town family and friends. Mark waited until they returned, prayed a blessing, and then picked up a glass of tea. Some of the ladies urged him to get a plate and he said he would when everyone else was eating. Gail came over and complimented him on the sermon. "I think it was just what Sammy would have wanted." She then asked if he still wanted to meet that afternoon or wait until another day. With the focus on the funeral, he had forgotten about their weekly meeting to discuss church correspondence and other administrative matters. This usually took about fifteen minutes on Monday afternoons. Gentry Baptist Church didn't require a lot of administrative action.

"Why don't we do it tomorrow? 3:00? Is that okay with you?" She replied it was and moved away to refill tea glasses. The others had filled their plates and were eating so he picked up a plate and looked over the choices. The food had been cooked by the ladies of the church and it all looked good. He got as much as his plate would hold and took a seat. Jeanette Bass came over and placed a large portion of coconut cake in front of him. "Last piece," she said. "I saved it for you." If he kept eating like this, he would have to buy larger waist pants.

When everyone finished and left the church, he started to walk home and remembered he had driven that morning. Returning to the church, he got in the Falcon and was about to drive when he noticed Gail, shaking her head and grinning at him. She knew he had forgotten about his car.

His little apartment was hot, and he turned the window fan on high, for what little good it did. Removing his clothes, he put on a pair of old shorts and lay down on the bed. He intended to rest but soon fell asleep. Awaking with a start, he looked at the clock. Five o'clock! When had he slept that long in the afternoon? Mrs. Cole would be home shortly and cook supper. After the meal he had at lunch, he really didn't need to eat again but didn't want her to waste food.

After supper, they moved to the screened porch and turned on the box fan. Their minds were filled with thoughts about the day but neither one said much. At 8:30, Mark excused himself and started off the porch. As he opened the screen, Mrs. Cole said, "Preacher, you did a really fine job today. I know you were worried because you hadn't ever done a funeral. That was one of the best, most appropriate funeral sermons I've ever heard."

He thanked her for the compliment and went down the

steps. Something caused him to turn and look at the pavement where the accident occurred. So much had happened in the last five days. Lives had been changed forever.

Chapter 6

A couple of weeks after he had become pastor of the Gentry Baptist Church, Gail Smith suggested that they meet for a few minutes each week and take care of any administrative issues. As church secretary/clerk she handled correspondence, ordered literature, and saw that the church bills were paid. At first, they tried to do this on Sunday before Sunday School, but there always seemed to be a distraction or someone needed Mark's attention.

Then they decided to meet briefly during the week and Monday afternoon was agreed on. Mark preferred to stay at home to study and prepare his sermons until after lunch. For a few weeks, they met at the church, usually no longer than thirty minutes. But one day they had several items to discuss and they previewed the church events for the upcoming months, which included Thanksgiving and Christmas. Since this was Mark's first experience with these events as a pastor, he had many questions about them. As they were leaving by the back door of the church, he was surprised to see that over three hours had elapsed.

As he turned to lock the door, he heard Gail softly say, "Uh oh. We are in trouble." Turning quickly, he asked why. She shushed him and quietly said, "Don't be too obvious, but glance across the road." Doing so he noticed a woman in her front yard staring across at them. "I don't understand" he said. "Why are we in trouble?" She said nothing but walked to the front of the church where the cars were parked. "That's Sadie Hightower. She's the town gossip. I imagine she was watching to see how long we would be in the church and she will make some gossip out of it."

Mark sputtered, "But...but, we weren't doing anything wrong! She has no reason to gossip." Shaking her head, Gail replied, "Sadie doesn't need a reason. She can take anything and make a story out of it. I'm sorry. I shouldn't have put you in this position." Mark shook his head. "Don't you blame yourself. Besides, maybe she won't say anything."

Gail had been correct in her assumption that Sadie Hightower would spread gossip about their long meeting in the church. By the end of the week her story had spread all over Gentry that the two of them had spent the entire afternoon in the church. JUST THE TWO OF THEM! Sadie

Hightower's greatest joy in life was to gossip, true or untrue, it didn't matter to her. She relished telling and re-telling-- and at times, embellishing--the gossip to anyone and everyone who would listen. Defamation of someone's character or reputation did not deter her.

When word of this reached Mark, he knew something different had to be done. They would need to meet in a public place where people could see them. The only place he could think of was the restaurant. Approaching Myrtle, he asked if it would inconvenience her if they met at the restaurant on Monday afternoons to handle the church business.

Myrtle readily agreed and then said, "I take it you heard Sadie Hightower's gossip." Mark groaned. He had hoped that few would hear it. "Why preacher, Sadie Hightower can spread gossip all over town while the truth is putting on its shoes. You and Gail aren't the first she's gossiped about and won't be the last."

"What can I do about it? I certainly wouldn't want to harm Miss Smith's character and reputation."

"You just did," she said with a grin. "By meeting here, you and Gail will show that you don't have anything to hide. This will put an end to her gossip about y'all. Cut her vine off at the root, so to speak."

They began meeting every Monday at the restaurant but

moved it to Tuesday due to the funeral on Monday. He was walking to the restaurant when he heard a horn and turned to see the green Comet pulling up to the curb. Stump leaned his head out of the window and said, "I'm going to call the Kelly's and see when's a good time to go over there. Probably be after 5:00, when Doyle gets home from work. You got any preference?"

"Thursday would be fine with me," Mark replied. "Okay, I'll let you know." Stump said as he pulled away from the curb. Mark went on to meet Gail at the restaurant. At lunch on Wednesday, Mrs. Cole passed on the message: Thursday at 5:00.

Mark was waiting on the porch Thursday when Stump pulled to the curb. He would have walked the few blocks to the Kelly's house, but Stump was averse to walking. Said he had taken the walking tour of Europe during the war and walked enough to last three lifetimes. Doyle Kelly met them at the door and ushered them into the living room where his wife, Wanda, sat on the couch. Sue Kelly sat in a chair, eyes red from crying. Wanda stood and directed the guests to take the couch and she went into the kitchen. Stump thanked them for their time, saying there were some unanswered questions about Sammy's death. "Was Sammy over here last Thursday night?" Doyle responded by telling them that he was working overtime at the paper mill and Sue had taken an unplanned trip to Valdosta to spend the night with some cousins. "So both of you were gone? You didn't see Sammy?"

"That's right," Doyle replied. "We thought he may have left here when he ran out into the highway," Stump said. Doyle turned to the kitchen and said, "Wanda, did Sammy come over here last Thursday night?" Keeping her back to them she replied, "Didn't see him."

Stump exhaled and slumped down a little. He was hopeful the Kelly's might know something. "It's just puzzling, real puzzling", he said. "Who would Sammy run from? What would cause him to run out in front of a car?" He reached to his shirt pocket for a cigarette but stopped, having a policy to not smoke in people's houses. Looking up at Doyle and Sue, he said, "One more question. Do you know what 'run...Joseph' could mean?" Father and daughter looked at one another quizzically and shook their heads no.

Stump stood and Mark followed suit. Stump thanked them again for their time and he said, "I know this is really hard, especially for you Sue." The girl nodded her head and tears began to flow.

Once in the car, Stump lit a cigarette and sat for a minute. "Preacher, this here is a real puzzle. There *has* to be an explanation, I just don't know what it is." The man did not have the training of a full-time policeman, but he had an inquisitive mind and a bulldog tenacity. If he were a betting man, Mark would bet Stump would get to the bottom of this puzzle.

After parking at the curb in front of the Cole house, he said, "Preacher, most folks think this was just a tragic accident. That maybe Sammy was in a hurry and didn't see the car. I'm convinced there's more to it. We won't talk about it but let's keep our eyes and ears open. If you see or hear anything that sounds like it may be connected to Sammy's death, let me know." After assuring him that he would, Mark went in the house where Edith Cole had supper waiting.

The nightmares started the next night. Sammy was in a dark, seemingly bottomless pit. Mark was lying chest down, reaching over the edge, holding Sammy by one hand, trying to pull him up and the boy was begging him not to let go. With great exertion, Mark was trying to pull the teenager out of the hole when his grip slipped and Sammy fell screaming down, down, down. Mark jumped awake, shaking all over. He got up, washed his face, and drank a glass of milk. Returning to bed, he tossed and turned for a long time, tormented by the nightmare.

Mark's nightmares continued. Sometimes he'd have two or three nightmares a week. Sometimes a couple of weeks would go by and Mark would get hopeful they were over. But they resumed.

Chapter 7

On Saturday afternoon, Mark drove to Valdosta to shop for that new suit he needed. Entering the Belk-Hudson store, his former boss, the manager of the men's department, greeted him cordially and asked what brought him to Valdosta. "I need a suit," Mark informed him. The manager led him to the suit rack and asked if he was looking for a specific color. "I have a blue and a gray."

"How about brown?" He found Mark's size in a medium brown and said, "I think you know where the dressing room is." Both laughed. Mark had been a good employee and the manager had hoped he would take a full-time job. The suit fit perfectly, and the pants were measured for alteration. Mark selected a matching tie and reached for his wallet when the manager said, "I don't know what you wear when you preach, but I've got some sport coats that are reduced. Good buys." Mark shrugged and was led to a rack of sport coats with a large Sale sign above it. The manager took a muted blue and burgundy plaid off the hanger and Mark tried it on. He liked it. As he tried on a pair of matching pants, he looked at his penny loafers and noticed how worn they looked. It was the only pair of shoes he owned besides a pair of tennis shoes. He paid for the clothes and was given a ticket to pick up the altered suit pants next week after alterations.

He then went to the shoe department and bought a pair of cordovan wing tips. As he left the store, he realized that he had spent over twice as much money as he had intended. No new clothes for a while, he told himself.

Still, he was in a good mood as he drove to Shoney's, intending to get a burger and strawberry pie. Pulling into the parking lot, he slowly circled, looking for a particular turquoise and white car. It wasn't there. He pulled into an empty parking spot and turned off his engine. That sense of loneliness swept over him. He admitted to himself that he hadn't come to Shoney's for food but hoping by some chance that Gail Smith might be there. She wasn't, and he was deeply disappointed. He had thoroughly enjoyed the time spent with her the previous Saturday and had hoped to see her again. Maybe Myrtle was right. Maybe he needed a wife. He remembered something Mark Twain wrote: *"To get the full value of joy you must have someone to divide it with."*

What was it about Gail Smith? She wasn't the prettiest girl he had known, although she was pretty in his opinion. Was it her personality?

He wasn't sure, but whatever it was, something about her appealed to him. And he wasn't quite sure *what* that something was. Could *she* be the woman he had waited for God to bring into his life? She hadn't done anything to indicate that she was. Or could his thoughts and feelings just be the result of loneliness? Suddenly, his appetite for a burger and strawberry pie subsided. He drove home and had a cold sandwich and a glass of milk for supper. Alone.

The next day, he wore the sport coat to church and received many compliments from the women as they entered the church. Then Gail Smith came in and said, "Nice coat. It really looks good on you." He felt his face turning red and for a moment was at a loss for words, finally stammering out a thank you. Why did he react that way? None of the other compliments bothered him.

He decided he would take the initiative and ask Gail to ride with him to Valdosta the following Saturday to pick up his pants, making certain he had some company. When he asked her on Wednesday night, she replied, "Oh Mark, I'd love to but my brother and his family from Tallahassee are coming this weekend. Perhaps some other time." He tried hard not to let his disappointment show.

After picking up his pants, he went to Shoney's for a burger, fries, and strawberry pie, eating in a booth by himself. For some reason, the food lacked taste. Looking around the restaurant, he couldn't help but notice the many couples eating, talking, laughing, and holding hands. What was that the Bible said? *"It is not good that man be alone: I will make him an help meet for him."*

Chapter 8

Mark was usually the first to arrive at the church on Sunday morning. Standing in the vestibule, he greeted his congregation as they arrived for Sunday School. He looked forward to this time and the interaction with the people. On the second Sunday of September, Paul and Hilda Slocum entered and asked if they could speak to him in private. Moving over to a corner of the sanctuary, he wondered what the problem could be. Worry was written all over their faces.

Paul Slocum was a big man, still fit at age sixty, and tan from working outdoors. He supervised the county road crews for the county that graded the numerous dirt roads. Mark waited for them to speak as Paul nervously turned his hat in his hands. Clearing his voice, he said, "Preacher, I've been having some tests done and they've found a spot on one of my lungs. They're fairly sure it's cancer. I'm having surgery

Tuesday at Shands Hospital in Gainesville. We didn't want to say anything until we knew for sure."

"Paul, I'm sorry to hear this. What do the doctors say?" The big man continued. "They think we caught it early enough but won't know until they operate. One of the doctors is from Gentry, Richard Cunningham. Grew up here. Anyway, he seems to think the operation will be successful." Paul then paused for a moment as if reluctant to continue talking. Glancing at Hilda, he said, "Uh, preacher, we were wondering if...if you..."

Mark read his mind. Paul wondered if he could be at the hospital for the surgery. "Paul, I will be there." A look of relief crossed their faces. "Thank you preacher. We don't have any family here and I didn't want Hilda there by herself. The surgery could take several hours." Mark asked what day and time. "This Tuesday at 7:00 AM. I know that's early. Hope it won't put you out too much." He assured them it would be fine. He then said, "Let me pray for you." After he finished his prayer, Paul and Hilda looked as if a huge burden had been lifted as they moved away to go to their Sunday School classes.

Mark's sermon that morning was from Mark 6, the storm on the Sea of Galilee. He made several points in the sermon:

(1)Jesus knew the storm was coming before the

disciples did.

(2)When they couldn't see him, Jesus knew where they were and the difficulty they were experiencing.

(3)When they couldn't get to Jesus, he came to them.

(4)When Jesus is with us, we don't have to be afraid.

Leaving church, Paul grabbed Mark's hand and shook it enthusiastically. "Preacher, that's just what I needed to hear today. How did you know to preach that sermon?" Of course, Mark had not known about it. He responded, "I didn't Paul, but God did." As they walked away, Mark silently thanked his heavenly Father for using him to meet the spiritual needs of people, even when he didn't know what was happening in their lives.

He was having dinner with the Wyman Hayes family. The members often invited him to eat with them. Invitations were usually extended after church so he seldom knew who he would be eating with. The children had finished eating and gone outside to play. As the adults chatted, he told them about Paul and asked how long it would take to drive to Gainesville. Wyman said about two hours to get to the hospital.

On his way home, he calculated when he needed to leave on Tuesday morning in order to be at the hospital before Paul's surgery, wanting to have prayer with him. Four o'clock, he thought. I'll have to get up at 4:00 in order to get there by 7:00. He could leave on Monday and spend the night in a motel. "Wish I knew someone in Gainesville," he said aloud.

Wait a minute! He did know someone in Gainesville-Bill and Emma Swain. They had attended Valdosta State College together and he had been an usher in their wedding. Bill was enrolled in law school at the University of Florida. Maybe, just maybe, he could spend Monday night with them. Sure would be easier than getting up at 4:00 in the morning.

Using Mrs. Cole's phone, he got the number, and dialed. Bill answered and Mark joked, "I hope I didn't wake you from your afternoon nap." After exchanging friendly insults, Mark told Bill about the situation and asked if it would be possible for him to spend Monday night with them. "Sure. If you don't mind sleeping on the couch. Our apartment is a one-bedroom, but the couch is roomy and comfortable. We'd love to see you." Mark then wrote down the directions. Bill said, "Why don't you come early Monday afternoon and I'll show you around Gainesville?" They settled on 3:00. "See you then." Mark was pleased. He wouldn't have to get up so early and he would see some old friends.

He and Bill greeted one another as only old friends can. Bill said he would be glad to show Mark some of the city and campus if he would drive. "We only have one car and Emma drives it to work. I ride my bike or walk to class." For the next hour or so, they took a leisurely drive around the city and campus. Bill showed him the football stadium and said, "You need to come to one of the games. We have a new quarterback this year, kid named Steve Spurrier, and man, can he throw the ball. And you remember Bruce Bennett, the kid who played quarterback for the Valdosta Wildcats? He's a defensive back and a good one."

Mark said he would like that. Bill said he would see about getting tickets and let him know. They returned to the apartment where Emma had prepared a simple but delicious meal. They sat up and talked until almost midnight. While at Valdosta State, they had rented apartments in the same house. It was built around 1900 and the owners had raised a large family. After their kids left, they made two apartments. Bill and Emma rented the larger apartment upstairs and Mark rented the small one downstairs. They became good friends, studying together, sharing many meals, playing tennis, and swimming at Twin Lakes. Mark often contributed to the meal budget and Emma graciously cooked enough to include him. They laughed about the "ton" of tuna casserole they had eaten. Bill asked, "What was that you would eat for breakfast?" Mark laughed and replied, "Peanut butter on toast with maple syrup. I didn't like to take time to cook breakfast but when Mom asked me if I were eating a hot breakfast, I could say 'yes' and be truthful. The toast was hot when I took it out of the toaster."

Bill finally said, "I could enjoy this all night, but I guess we better go to bed. All of us have long days tomorrow." The next morning, Mark dressed as quietly as he could, slipped out, and drove the short distance to the hospital. Getting directions, he went to the area where Paul was being prepped for surgery. Their faces broke into broad smiles when he entered. There was enough time for a short conversation and then he prayed just before Paul was taken to the operating room. He and Emma went to the cafeteria for breakfast, although she didn't eat much.

By 8:00 they were settled in the waiting room. The doctor had said the surgery could last until noon. Trying to distract her from worry, he asked about their family. Her face brightened as she talked about their son, Paul Jr., who was in the army, stationed at Fort Benning, Georgia. "He wanted to be here but couldn't get away. He's a drill instructor. Been in nine years and will probably make a career out of it. He and his wife have three children." Her face beamed with pride and it was obvious she loved her son and his family.

"Any more children?" he asked. The way Emma dropped her head made him regret asking the question. Sadness replaced the joy on her face. "Yes, a daughter named

Deborah." He asked where Deborah lived and the answer was, they didn't know. "She was always a rebellious child, Preacher. Slipping around smoking and drinking while she was still in high school and getting in trouble. She dropped out of school and got married. It didn't last. She was working as a waitress at the Flamingo restaurant in Tadlock when she run off with a truck driver. That was five years ago, and we haven't heard from her since." She stopped talking and Mark knew this was a painful subject for her to discuss.

Leaning back in the chair, it occurred to him that there was much he did not know about his congregation, and possibly never would. He realized that there were people who never talked about their grief and sorrows. They just lived with it. People like Nell Garber who carried the burden of losing those she loved the most. People like Emma and Paul wounded by a wayward child. How many more in his congregation carried their burdens silently? Preacher, he said to himself, you have a lot to learn about being a pastor and a comforter to hurting people.

A couple of times, Mark walked around the hospital, visited the gift shop, and went for a cup of coffee. Emma would not leave the waiting area except to go to the restroom. This was Mark's first experience waiting with someone who had a loved one in surgery. He was amazed at how emotionally tiring the waiting could be. Another lesson learned he told himself.

At 11:55, the doctor came out and reported that the surgery was complete. Paul would be in recovery for about an hour and then Emma could see him. Apprehensively she asked about the surgery. "It was a small area, malignant, but I think we got it all. We won't know for sure until the reports come back in about a week." Mark asked how long Paul would be hospitalized and the answer was five to seven days. The doctor excused himself. Emma's relief was apparent. "Why don't we have a prayer of thanksgiving," Mark said. At lunch, Emma ate more heartily. After visiting Paul, still groggy from the anesthesia, Mark left to return home.

Paul returned home in a few days. The surgery was successful, but the doctor forbade him to smoke. In a month he was the healthy robust man he had always been, and a new bond had developed between Mark and the Slocum's. They often hosted him for Sunday dinner and Paul took him fishing.

Chapter 9

It was Thursday, October 1, 1964. As Mark flipped the page of the Liberty National Life Insurance calendar to October, he could not have foreseen that three events in the coming month would have great impact on his life and ministry.

The first one occurred on Sunday. It was his routine to walk to the vestibule while the deacon of the week prayed the benediction. He would greet the worshipers as they filed out, usually hearing compliments or comments about the sermon. Stella Boyd was one of the first to come out. She had a definite look of disapproval on her face. In a critical tone of voice, she said, "Getting rather carried away with your preaching aren't you? I didn't know we had called a Pentecostal to be our preacher!" Mark was so flabbergasted he couldn't respond. It was an awkward moment for anyone within hearing distance. Stella tossed her head and walked out. Almost nothing was said by the remaining worshipers as they filed out.

When the church was empty, Mark walked to the back pew and sat down, bewildered. Why had Stella said what she said, he wondered? One thing was for sure--he was in Stella Boyd's doghouse. The Sunday night attendance was smaller than usual, and they were subdued.

He met with Gail on Monday afternoon and she seemed distracted. After finishing their business, she closed her folder and said, "Mark, are you aware that Stella Boyd has been calling the members, complaining about your preaching, and saying it's time to get a new preacher?" He was dumbfounded. No, he wasn't aware of it. Gail continued. "Mark, she's our church troublemaker. I've been a member of this church all my life and I've seen her in action before. She's been responsible for running off more than one preacher, or at least, making his life so miserable he left. What are you going to do?"

Shaking his head, he replied, "I don't know." And that was the truth. *He didn't know what to do.*

On Wednesday night, Gail's mother asked him to have lunch with her the next day. Sunday meal invitations were commonplace, but this was his first invitation for a weekday meal. "Come about 11:00 and we can talk." He had a restless night, wondering how this would end. "You may establish a new record for the shortest pastorate in the Southern Baptist Convention," he said to himself.

The Smith house was one mile south of Gentry on State Road 243. The house sat about 100 yards off the paved road on a 300-acre farm. After Mr. Smith's stroke, Mrs. Smith had leased the farmland to a neighbor. As he pulled up the long driveway, he was relieved that no other cars were in sight. At least it wasn't a lynching party.

Mrs. Smith greeted him and ushered him into the neat living room, motioning for him to take a seat. He had been here once before when they hosted him for Sunday dinner. "Preacher," she said, "Let's not beat around the bush. You know that Stella Boyd is trying to get you dismissed as our pastor."

"Yes ma'am."

"She is offended by what she refers to as your theatrics when you preach." Theatrics? That's not how Mark thought of his preaching. It was true that his preaching style had changed since he had become the pastor of the Gentry Baptist Church. At first, his delivery had been somewhat formal. He stood behind the pulpit, hardly moving during the sermon. He modulated his voice but never got loud. That had changed. Now he moved around on the platform, occasionally coming down to the floor level. And he did raise his voice as he emphasized a crucial statement in his sermon.

"Preacher tell me why you are preaching the way you are now. Why have you changed?" Mark paused, wanting to give the correct answer to her question. He couldn't help but wonder if she agreed with Stella Boyd. He pondered for a moment before answering. "I could give several reasons, all of which would be valid, but I guess it comes down to two things. First, Sammy Garber's death has changed me. I've come to realize the absolute truth of what the Bible says about life. It is short, it is fragile, and it can end at any time. Our life is a vapor as James puts it. And second, more than ever I'm committed to the gospel that forgives sin and saves souls. To me, it's something I need to be passionate about. Sin is serious and eternity is long."

He paused to draw a breath and then continued. "I can't be lukewarm as the Bible says. When I start to preach now, there is an urgency that comes over me. I can't help it, I can't control it, and to be truthful, I don't want to. I want God to use me and if that means being theatrical, as Stella puts it, then that's how I'll have to be. I'm just sorry that this is causing problems within the church."

"You aren't doing any of this to call attention to yourself are you?", she asked. Mark was appalled. "No ma'am! I never want to call attention to myself in the pulpit. Nothing needs to detract from the gospel and from Jesus."

When he finished, Mrs. Smith looked at him with a look he couldn't discern. He didn't know if she didn't believe him, didn't agree with him, or what. After what seemed like a small eternity she spoke. "Preacher, I can see your point and for what it's worth, I am in total agreement. Now, how are you going to handle this with the congregation? You must do something, or Stella will continue to stir up trouble."

Mark stared out the window and then softly replied, "I don't know. I just don't know."

"Well, we are going to pray about it and I'm sure God will give you the guidance you need. Now, let's eat." As he followed her to the dining room, he was wishing he could be as optimistic as she was. Over their meal, his tension eased, and he enjoyed the food and the company of this dear, sweet lady, who just happened to be Gail's mother.

"Gail tells me your mother lives in Athens. It would be nice for her to come visit sometime," she said. Mark hadn't thought of his mother coming to visit Gentry. That was something he needed to pursue.

When he returned to his apartment, he sat down at the dinette table and began to pray for wisdom and guidance. "Heavenly Father, you are not surprised by what is happening and I believe that you can lead me to the right solution, the Biblical solution. Father help me to behave as I should. That no matter what is done or said, help me demonstrate the qualities that Jesus did when he was persecuted." He would repeatedly pray for wisdom and guidance until Sunday morning.

After the Sunday morning service, he did not go to the vestibule as he normally did. He returned to the pulpit and asked everyone to be seated for a moment. He began by apologizing for any misunderstanding or offense he may have committed. Stella Boyd had a smug look on her face. Clearing his throat, he essentially repeated what he had told Mrs. Smith on Thursday. "Now, I have prayed about this and I do not wish to be offensive or be a distraction in any way as you worship. I am ready to offer my resignation as your pastor."

An obvious turmoil swept over the congregation. Harley Bass was the deacon of the week and had been sitting on the front pew waiting to pray the benediction. He jumped up and walked to the pulpit. "Preacher, I have something to say. Folks, when we called this man to be our pastor, I was personally convinced he was a man of God. In the four months he has been here, he has affirmed my belief in many ways. Any change in him has been a change for the better." That was a long speech for Harley Bass.

Nell Garber stood and voiced her support for Mark. Others followed. Mark was moved by their expressions of support and affirmation of his preaching. Seeing that the tide was turning against her, Stella Boyd arose and said, "He gave his resignation and I make a motion we accept it." To his surprise, Mrs. Smith stood. "No Stella, he did not resign. He said he was ready to resign. There's a difference. He did not officially resign. Besides, this isn't an official business meeting."

Harley Bass had sat down but now stood and said, "This is not an official vote but as Chairman of the Deacons, I think we need to support our pastor and show him we want him to stay. All who support him and want him to stay, raise your hands." Every hand in the building went up except for Stella's and five or six of her crowd. Then the congregation broke into a spontaneous applause. Stella Boyd jumped to her feet and quickly exited the church.

People left their seats and came to Mark with handshakes, hugs, and words of encouragement. When Mrs. Smith hugged him, she whispered, "I knew our Lord would tell you what to do." He whispered a "thank you" in her ear. Gail did not hug him or say anything. She just held his hand for a moment, but her eyes spoke volumes. Stella and her friends did not attend church again and within weeks, joined another church.

~

The second event that would impact his life was a phone call from Bill Swain. Mark and Mrs. Cole had just finished eating supper when the phone rang. She was washing dishes and asked Mark if he would answer the phone. He immediately recognized Bill's voice. "Are you ready for a football game?" his friend asked. "I have tickets for the South Carolina game, Saturday the 17th. Can you make it?" Mark affirmed that he could. "Come on down early and we can have lunch before the game." He was excited. It had been years since he had attended a college football game. Once a year, he and his father would attend a University of Georgia game. Zeke Bratkowski, the outstanding Bulldog quarterback who went on to star in the NFL, was his favorite player.

Florida was off to a good start, having won their first three games, and expectations were high for a winning season and a bowl game. Bill had not exaggerated about Steve Spurrier. He was a proficient passer, kicked extra points and field goals, and was an outstanding punter. Florida dominated the game and won, 37-0. To Mark, one of the entertaining things was "Mr. Two Bits." He was a fan who moved around the stadium, going from section to section, leading the Florida fans in a cheer. It was entertaining just to watch Mr. Two Bits lead the cheer.

Two Bits!

Four Bits!

Six Bits!

A Dollar!

All for the Gators,

Stand up and holler!

Walking back to Bill's apartment, they talked about the game and then Bill asked him how things were going in his life. "Okay I guess," Mark replied. "Are you dating anyone?" Mark started to give an evasive answer when Bill suddenly pointed his finger and said, "Don't you prevaricate!" They both doubled over laughing. Prevaricate was a favorite word of a professor at Valdosta State. When any student would start to give an excuse for not completing an assignment, the professor would point his finger and say, "Now don't you prevaricate." Most students had to resort to the dictionary to know what he meant. Catching his breath, Mark said, "Boy, that brings back memories."

As they continued their walk, Bill asked the question again. Mark stopped and looked his friend squarely in the face. "Bill, I live in a small town, where there is only one unmarried female anywhere near my age."

"Okay," Bill said. "Is she attractive?"

"Yes. I would call her attractive?"

"Does she date anyone?", Bill continued.

"No."

"Have you asked her for a date?"

"No."

"Then, my single, twenty-five-year-old friend, is there any reason you shouldn't ask her for a date?" Mark shook his head. No there wasn't. Playfully stabbing his finger in Mark's chest, he said, "The next time I see you, I want to hear that you asked her for a date. Got it?" Grinning, Mark said, "Okay."

On his ride home, he thought over what Bill had challenged him to do. True, there wasn't any reason *not* to ask Gail for a date. His dilemma was *how* to ask her.

~

The third event that impacted his life in October was the school Halloween carnival. In a small town like Gentry, school events were really community events. Ballgames, carnivals, school plays--they were a part of the social life in Gentry. Several of the kids in church made a point to invite him to the carnival. Halloween fell on Saturday and the school grounds were busy all day with students, teachers, and other volunteers getting ready.

It was almost dark when Mark strolled over to the school. He was somewhat surprised at the amount of work that had been done. Poles had been erected for the booths and old bed sheets, sheets of burlap (called tobacco sheets in Gentry) and butcher paper had been nailed or stapled to the poles to partition off sections for the classes to use. A tractor pulled a flatbed trailer with hay for the hayride. The smaller kids were lined up at a booth where they used a fishing pole to "fish" for a prize. There was quite a variety of games and contests: dart throw, the apple bob, baseball throw to knock down empty milk bottles, and many others. Mark saw a sign pointing to a haunted house and heard the screams of frightened kids. It brought back memories of the school carnival in Bishop when he was a kid.

Sally Hayes, Wyman's teenage daughter, grabbed him and pulled him over to the cake walk. Buying his tickets, he joined the contestants. Various women had baked cakes and donated them for the cake walk. Music would play, the contestants would walk in a circle, stopping when the music stopped, and the person standing at a marked spot won the cake. Mark walked through several sequences of the music and was announced as the winner of the cake. Someone handed him a delicious looking chocolate frosted cake. Gail happened to walk by, and he said, "Look, I've won a cake!" She stopped and replied, "That's not just any cake. That's one of Trudy Paramore's ten-layer yellow cakes with homemade chocolate frosting. You will never eat a better cake than that."

Studying the cake, he said, "I'll never eat all of this. Why don't you and your mother take it. You can give me a slice or two." She paused for a moment and replied, "Tell you what. I'll take the cake home and you eat with us Sunday. That can be our dessert." How could he refuse an offer like that? She pointed out her car and asked him to put the cake on the front seat. Someone was calling "Miz Gail" to assist in one of the booths.

Something noticeable was happening at the Gentry Baptist Church—an increase in attendance. No one knew for sure why it was happening, but it was happening. Some believed it was because of Mark's preaching. Perhaps it was a result of his visitation efforts to the unchurched in Gentry. And some secretly believed it was because Stella Boyd no longer attended the church. Since her departure, the whole congregation seemed more energized.

After the Sunday morning service, he drove to the Smith home in an upbeat frame of mind. Things had certainly changed for the better since he was last there. After a delicious meal of roast beef, mashed potatoes, vegetables, and biscuits so light and fluffy Mark wondered how they stayed on the plate, he was stuffed. There was no way he could eat dessert. Mrs. Smith seemed to read his mind. "Why don't we wait a while to eat dessert. You two go sit on the front porch while I clean off the table." They insisted on helping but she was insistent they go sit on the porch. "Besides, it'll only take a minute."

Mark and Gail took seats in comfortable rocking chairs. As he gently rocked, he felt a rare peace and contentment. Then a little voice in his head said, *"There will never be a better time!"* Without looking at her he asked if she would like to go to a movie next Saturday. When she responded with a yes, he had to control his excitement. Stealing a sideways glance, he could see a hint of a smile on Gail's face. Mrs. Smith came and joined them on the porch. "After a while, I'll make some coffee and we'll eat some of Trudy's cake." She then drew Mark into conversation about his background. He told her about his parents and of growing up in Bishop, Georgia, a place much like Gentry. "I know where Bishop is," she said. "We used to go through there on our way to Cashiers, North Carolina."

This was somewhat of a revelation to Mark. "You've been through Bishop?" She continued. "Oh yes. When Gail's father was alive, we vacationed every year in Cashiers." Looking at

Gail, he said, "I didn't know you had been through Bishop." Arching one eyebrow she replied, "There's lots you don't know about me." He thought it wise not to respond to that comment. "When y'all passed through Bishop, you were about two miles from our house." A memory caused him to chuckle. "When I was a kid playing with my friends, we would stand on the sidewalk and wave at the cars passing through town. It was a form of entertainment to us." Mrs. Smith clapped her hands and laughed. "I remember seeing kids do that! Joe would toot his horn and we would wave back. Just think Gail, you may have waved at the preacher when y'all were children." Gail retorted, "What I think is that you two are going way too far with your imagination," which elicited another round of laughter from her mother and Mark. The conversation continued for another hour and then Mrs. Smith went to make the coffee. "Now that's something to consider," Mark said. When Gail asked what, he replied, "That we could have waved at each other as children and now we know each other as adults." Gail was thinking that it was possible. A call from inside summoned them to cake and coffee. When he had finished a large slice of cake he told Gail that she was right. That was perhaps the best cake he had ever eaten. Mark would have stayed longer but excused himself to go home and prepare for the evening worship service.

Euphoria would be an inadequate word to describe his

mood as he drove home. He had done it! He had asked Gail for a date and she had accepted. He had dated many times before, but this was a whole new level. There was something about Gail Smith that made all other dates pale in comparison. Just wait until he saw Bill Swain again!

The evening worship service was good. Attendance was increasing, the singing was enthusiastic, and Mark was energized for his sermon. Arriving home in a good mood, he ate a peanut butter and jelly sandwich with a glass of milk and then read a book he had checked out from the mobile library that came to town each week. He read until he was sleepy and went to bed, wondering how life could be any better than it was today. Sometime after midnight, he had the nightmare which woke him up. He always woke up from the nightmare when Sammy slipped from his grasp and fell screaming down into the dark, bottomless pit. Sitting on the side of the bed, he wondered how long they would continue. Would Sammy Garber's death always haunt him?

Chapter 10

Mark and Gail started what became a routine—driving to Valdosta every Saturday afternoon for a matinee movie followed by a meal at Shoney's. There developed a comfort in the relationship with neither one feeling they had to act a certain way or impress one another. November was a quiet month compared to the previous three. Mark spent his mornings preparing sermons, visited the members who required hospitalization, usually in Tadlock and occasionally in Valdosta, and continued inviting unchurched people to worship.

Coming home after their third date, Mark stopped his car and was reaching for the door when Gail placed her hand on his arm. "Mark, wait a minute. There's something I need to tell you and I hope it doesn't disappoint you." His heart sank. She was going to end their dating. "Mark, I really enjoy our time together and I would like for it to continue the way it is for now." Inwardly he breathed a huge sigh of relief. She continued. "When I was in college, I had a very disappointing romance, dating someone for almost two years. I thought I was in love and then discovered he wasn't the person he pretended to be. I promised myself that the next time, I would be more certain about a man. Mark, we are mature adults, not a couple of teenagers motivated by passion or hormones. If it's okay with you, we will continue to date without jumping into romance."

She stopped and removed her hand from his arm, awaiting his response. "Gail, I am in complete agreement. I have never had a serious relationship because I'm still waiting for God to bring that one special person into my life. We will continue our dating without any commitment on either part." With a smile he said, "The Thomas men are not known for jumping into romantic relationships. The first time my dad kissed my mother was after the preacher pronounced them husband and wife." She laughed and said, "That may be taking it a bit too far." He got out, walked around to open her door, and escorted her up the steps. They spoke a "Goodnight" and a "See you tomorrow."

Mark made an extra effort to visit the church members who were incapacitated and unable to attend the worship services. In making those visits, he discovered a remarkable truth: he visited with the intent of blessing the person who was homebound but usually he felt that he had been blessed. There was widow Stewart who had battled a variety of health issues for years. When he made his monthly visit, she would bring him up to date on her health, not in a complaining way but just informing him. After giving him an update, she would always pause and then, with a smile on her face say, "But preacher, God's been so good to me." Every time he heard her say that, Mark would feel just a little bit of aggravation towards those members who would moan and groan about a bad cold.

Howard and Tilly Fry had been staunch members of the Gentry Baptist Church for decades. Age and disease were taking its toll on them. Howard was terribly arthritic but could have attended church if not for Tilly's condition. She had survived cancer, was severely diabetic, blind, and had dementia. More than one church member had told Mark they wish he could have known Tilly in her prime. She was the church pianist, taught Sunday School, and led the Vacation Bible School each year for longer than anyone could remember. No one could match her spiritual enthusiasm and physical energy.

Tilly was confined to bed and Howard had to attend to her every need. While Mark was visiting one day, Howard was trying to wash some food residue off her face. She began to curse him, using some very profane language which embarrassed Mark, not for himself but for Howard. When Tilly finished her tirade, Howard bent over, kissed her on the forehead, and said, "Now sweetheart, I know you didn't mean that." Mark's feeling of embarrassment was replaced by a sense of wonder. He had seen a true demonstration of the kind of love Paul wrote about in 1 Corinthians 13.

Interaction with his members provided learning experiences that could not be matched in a classroom nor learned by reading a book. He quickly learned which members should not be asked how they were feeling. It was an open invitation to hear about every ailment known to man.

He also learned about the ugliness of man's sin and vices. Janie Lane and her five small children frequently attended church, but her husband Elmer did not. Gail told him Elmer had a drinking problem, was anti-church, and could be mean when he was drinking. Stump Harris had to take him out of Mac's Bar on several occasions. Elmer owned a truck and hauled wood to the pulp mill. His income was barely enough for a family of seven, made worse by what he spent on alcohol. Mark could well imagine what the home life was like because the father of one of his school friends was an alcoholic. The family wore ragged clothes, drove a battered car, and sometimes lacked food. Mark's mother often invited his friend to eat with them.

When he raised the possibility of visiting Elmer, Janie begged him not to. He made a point of praying daily for Elmer, asking for guidance and direction on how to make a connection and possibly help the man. Somewhere he had read the statement: *You need to talk to God about a person before you talk to the person about God.*

Shortly after he began praying for Elmer, he chanced to meet him at the post office, introduced himself, and made small talk about his children. Elmer was reserved but seemed pleased when Mark spoke positively about his children. Thereafter, it seemed that the two men encountered one another frequently. Mark was friendly and avoided any mention of church to Elmer. Over time, Elmer warmed to Mark and would take the initiative to speak or call a greeting across the street. Leaving church one Sunday, Janie thanked him for being a friend to Elmer. "You are the first preacher he's ever liked," she told him.

As Mark walked past Cowen's gas station one day, he saw Elmer's truck and stopped to speak. The truck was loaded with wood indicating he was going to the pulp mill south of Valdosta. On a whim, Mark asked if he could ride along. When Elmer hesitated, Mark said he had never seen a pulp mill and was curious as to how it operated, and Elmer agreed. Several people stopped to stare when Elmer drove away with the preacher as a passenger.

During the half-hour drive to the mill, Mark asked questions about the pulpwood business. Elmer mentioned that he had learned to drive trucks in the Army, which led to a discussion of their military experiences. The more they talked, the more Elmer relaxed.

When Elmer checked his load into the mill yard, the workers greeted him with some unsavory language. Elmer quickly introduced Mark as "our preacher" which served to change the choice of words as well as surprise the preacher. On the ride back to Gentry, Elmer insisted on buying Mark a soft drink. As they got back in the truck, Elmer looked at him and said, "Preacher, I've got a question. Why haven't you ever said anything to me about church or the Lord.? Other preachers have hounded me about attending church. And another thing, don't you know about my drinking? Why have you been so friendly to me? I would think you wouldn't want to have anything to do with me."

Mark took a breath and silently prayed for God to give him the right words to respond. "Elmer, let me ask you a question. How would you have responded if I had 'hounded you' about church?" Taking a swallow of soft drink, he replied, "Wouldn't have had anything to do with you." Nodding, Mark continued, "I figured that, so I didn't 'hound you' as you say." Deciding to be bold, Mark asked, "Elmer, do you have any friends? I mean, real friends? Not the men you drink with at Mac's Bar." There was a long silence before the answer. "No, I don't." Mark sensed a tone of loneliness in the man's answer.

"Elmer, I won't lie. I do want to invite you to church and I would like to see you change for the better. But you were skeptical of me and my intentions since I was a preacher. I figured I needed to be your friend first and then we could talk about God and the church. That's all I'm trying to do--be your friend and, one day, maybe you will want to talk about God and the church. I certainly hope so."

Taking another swallow of his soft drink, Elmer said, "You're sure putting yourself out on a limb, trying to be my friend." Looking at Mark he grinned and said, "No telling what kind of talk there will be about you riding with me." Mark took a swallow and replied, "Elmer, let me tell you something. Jesus was criticized because he made friends of sinners, went to their houses, and ate with them. It really doesn't bother me if I'm criticized for being your friend."

Elmer was still for a minute and then cranked the truck and drove on to Gentry. As he stopped to let Mark out, he extended his hand and with a firm grip said, "Thanks preacher."

Elmer was right! There was considerable conversation in

Gentry about the strange friendship between the preacher and pulpwood man. Even Gail asked him about it. "Gail, would you agree that Elmer has had more than enough people criticize his lifestyle and vices?"

"Well...yes, I suppose so." He continued. "Don't you think he needs someone to be his friend, to be a positive influence in his life?" Before she could answer he said, "The Bible says that Jesus was a friend of sinners. And what was the title of that song you sang a couple of Sundays ago?"

"Jesus! what a Friend for Sinners!"

"Right. The bottom line is, do we just sing and preach about it or do we practice it?"

Gail threw up her hands in mock surrender. "Okay, okay, Reverend Thomas." Behind the smile on her face was a newfound respect for her pastor.

Myrtle Johns had her own perspective on the strange friendship and told him, "We've never had a preacher like you in this town, and maybe that's a good thing. A few weeks later, Elmer came to church with Janie and the children and word got around town that Mac's Bar had lost one of its regular customers.

And Mark discovered how generous some people could be. Ralph Kendall owned the Gentry Garage and worked on most folks' cars, trucks, and farm equipment. The residents of Gentry said that if it had a motor, Ralph could fix it. Periodically, Ralph would send Mark word to stop by the garage. Having learned of someone with a financial need, he would hand Mark some folded-up bills with the instructions to go visit the family and give them the money. The instructions always ended with the words, "And preacher, if you tell'em where the money came from, I'll have to kill ya." And then he would grin. Mark never counted it, so he had no idea just how much money Ralph distributed to the needy in and around Gentry and wanted no credit for it.

One Sunday, as Nell Garber spoke to Mark after church, she told him someone--she didn't know who--had paid for a headstone for Sammy's grave. She was pleased because she couldn't afford one but puzzled at who would do such a generous thing. The next time he saw Ralph Kendall, he mentioned it and the garage owner simply smiled and said, "Yeah, I heard about that." Mark had a fairly good idea of who had paid for the stone.

Mark's mother wrote him asking if he could possibly come to Athens for Thanksgiving. He answered by telling her that time would not permit it. He would have to drive up on Wednesday and return on Friday, allowing only one day to be with her. And to a point, that was true. What he did not tell her was that he was spending Thanksgiving with Gail and her family. He had not mentioned his relationship with Gail to his mother. At this point, they were just dating; and the relationship might end, although he fervently hoped it wouldn't. It was becoming increasingly more difficult *not* to think about Gail. He envisioned her face almost every moment of his waking hours. She was the first thing on his mind when he awoke and the last thing on his mind before he fell asleep.

The residents of Gentry were aware that the two were dating, and there was general approval. Gail, of course, was "hometown" and beloved by most everyone. In the short time he had been in Gentry, Mark had been accepted by most of the people. At church, they tried to keep the relationship in the background. He treated her as he would any other member. Only when alone did they call each other by their first names. In public, she called him Pastor or Rev. Thomas and he called her Miss Smith.

Gail's brother, Robert, his wife June, and their kids, Bobby, Ellen, and Linda came for Thanksgiving. Robert worked for a bank in Tallahassee and was ten years older than Gail. In the afternoon, the two men took the kids and walked around the farm. The entire day was a pleasant experience, even though Mark felt a twinge of guilt about not going to Athens.

The first Friday of December was the opening game of

the basketball season. Word got out that something special would be done before the game which resulted in a larger crowd than normal attending the game. The principal had requested that Nell Garber attend the game. When Sammy played, she never missed but now, she wasn't sure she would be able to attend the games. The principal told her it was important that she come, even if she didn't think she'd stay and watch the game.

The crowd watched the teams warm up, eagerly curious about the special thing that was to happen. Shortly before game time, the time-out horn sounded to get everyone's attention, and the principal walked to the center of the court and motioned for quiet. "As most of you know, this season would have been Sammy Garber's senior year. Unfortunately, we lost Sammy in that tragic accident." A stillness came over the gymnasium. Mark noticed the opposing team was still, listening to the principal. "A few weeks ago, the boys came to Coach Stovall and me with a request that we have agreed to and tonight, we share it with you. Mrs. Garber, would you step down here please?" Nervously, Nell Garber stood, and people moved to allow her access to the floor level. Coach Stovall met her and escorted her to center court. The principal continued. "Mrs. Garber, Sammy's teammates have requested that this season be dedicated to him." He paused and motioned for the team, who moved to center court carrying something wrapped in butcher paper. "And, that his jersey number be retired, meaning it won't ever be worn again." The paper was removed revealing Sammy's jersey, mounted, and framed. Two of the players hoisted it above their heads and slowly turned so that everyone in the gymnasium could see it. For a moment there was complete silence and then the stands erupted in cheers and applause. The sound continued for what seemed like several minutes and was almost deafening. It was an emotional event for everyone present, even the opposing team and their fans. People cheered, clapped, cried, and smiled—all at the same time. The sound echoed off the block walls of the gymnasium and far exceeded the celebration for any game ever won on that court.

When the clapping and cheering subsided, Nell Garber was escorted back to her seat and the teams readied for the game. Two thoughts occupied Mark's mind: The first was, how fitting this tribute was to honor the memory of Sammy Garber; and the second was that possibly someone in the gymnasium knew something about his death. He didn't see Stump Harris but was certain he was in the crowd somewhere and was thinking the same thing. Maybe, just maybe, they would learn something that would explain what led to Sammy's death.

The game itself was a good, close one with the lead changing several times. Gentry's best player fouled out in the middle of the fourth quarter and the Panthers lost by three points.

The next day, Mark and Gail went to a movie and to Shoney's. As they discussed the recognition for Sammy Garber, he decided to tell her about his nightmares. When he finished, she reached across the table and took his hand. "Oh, Mark, I'm so sorry. I guess Sammy's death affected you more than most."

"No," he replied, "no one is affected more than his mother." Since Sammy's death, Mark had seen the effects of grief and sorrow in Nell Garber. It showed on her face and in her posture. "You're right. At lunch, I see her gazing across the cafeteria, watching the kids eat, and I know she's missing Sammy. She told me one day that she hadn't done a thing to his room. It's just like it was the day he died. Is that odd?"

"I don't suppose it is," he replied. "People deal with their grief in different ways. Some want to move on with their lives and others need time. When my dad died, my mother waited a few weeks and then got rid of his clothes and some other things. To her, those things were painful reminders of what she had lost. Of course, she kept photos. She keeps a photo of the last wedding anniversary they celebrated on a table by her bed. A few months after he died, she said what pained her most was not having his clothes to wash each week."

Shaking her head, Gail said, "That's funny. My mother did almost the same thing when daddy died, and she also said that she missed his clothes in the wash." Mark responded, "You know, I'll bet there're a lot of similarities between our mothers."

"Mark, I would like to meet your mother sometime." During the conversation, she had continued to hold Mark's hand. He reached his other hand and enclosed her hand in both of his. "So, would I Gail. In fact, I've been thinking of a way to get her to come and visit but there's no room for her to stay with me. I've thought about asking Mrs. Cole if she could use her extra bedroom."

Now Gail extended her other hand and placed it on top of his. "She can stay with us. We have plenty of room."

"Are you sure? Would it be okay with your mother?"

"Yes, I'm sure, and yes, it would be okay with mother. We were talking about you the

other night and she said how nice it would be to meet your mother."

"Oh, so you're talking about me, huh?" Gail's face reddened a little and she replied, "Yes, we do." Mark said, "I hope it's all good." She smiled but did not respond.

Walking to the car, they held hands for the first time.

On the drive home, they discussed his mother's visit. "Why not Christmas?" Mark considered it and replied, "You know, that may be a good time. Aunt Catherine won't be alone because her children live close to her and they get together at Christmas. I can call her this week and see if she wants to come."

"How about tomorrow?" Gail asked. "You can eat dinner with us and use our phone to call her." He couldn't argue with that. When Mrs. Smith approached him before Sunday School, a smile covered her face. "Mark," she said, "Gail told me about your mother coming to visit and I think it's wonderful." That was the first time she had called him by his first name. It was always "Preacher", or "Reverend Thomas." He liked the sound of it. And she sounded as if his mother's visit was already planned.

It seemed that every Sunday the worship services got better. Or was it just him? Gail had a solo that morning and his message was about the Old Testament prophecy of the birth of Jesus Christ. A family Mark had been visiting joined the church. He was in high spirits as he drove to the Smith house for dinner.

During the meal they discussed the details of his mother's visit. Christmas would be on a Friday. Mrs. Smith suggested that she come and stay for several days, once again calling him by his first name. She didn't seem to be aware that she was doing it. "She could come a few days before Christmas and stay through Sunday, attend church and hear you preach."

"Mrs. Smith, I really appreciate your offer to let Mother stay here and it would be nice to have her stay several days. Bu, I don't want to impose..." He didn't get to finish the sentence. Dismissing the notion with a wave of her hand, she replied. "It's no trouble at all. Gail and I have talked it over and we want her to stay with us." He wondered what else they had talked over. It seemed apparent they had made some definite plans for his mother's visit.

After the meal, he moved to the living room to call his mother. He was excited about her coming. Now he was thinking like it was a certainty! His Aunt Catherine answered the phone and he had to chat with her a minute. When his mother took the phone, she asked if there was anything wrong. "No mom," he said, "there's nothing wrong. Mom, how would you like to come to Gentry for Christmas. Spend maybe a week here?"

There was a silence and he knew what she was doing. His mother had always been a deliberative person, never responding to anything quickly. Knowing that she was pondering his invitation, he added, "A family in our church has graciously offered to host you. They are wonderful people and I want you to meet them."

The silence continued. He was beginning to wonder if the call had been disconnected when she answered. "So, that means I could come down on Tuesday, the 22nd, and stay until Tuesday, the 29th?" He told her that would be fine. "And who is this family I would be staying with?", she asked.

"They are church members, Gail Smith and her mother."

"And does her mother have a name?"

"Yes ma'am, it's Rebecca. They have become special friends."

There was a silence and then she said, "And you and Gail are seeing one another, right?" How did mothers *always* know these things? He meekly replied, "Yes, ma'am," and braced himself for the next question. She was a relentless questioner, many times asking question after question to get the whole story of something that had happened when he was a kid. After another silence, she said, "Okay son, I'll see you on the 22nd."

"That's great Mom. We can't wait to see you."

She told him she would get a map and asked how long the drive would be. Knowing that she wouldn't drive on the Interstate, he said, "Mom, getting a map would be a good thing but it's really simple. Follow US 129 to Ray City, then go to Valdosta. From Valdosta, take US 41 South and you will come to Gentry. Probably take about seven hours." She told him to hold on and he knew she was getting a pen. "Okay, US 129 to Ray City, then to Valdosta and then US 41 South to Gentry."

"That's right Mom."

"Okay son, I'll see you then. Goodbye. I love you Son."

"I love you too Mom. Goodbye."

Hanging up the phone, he expelled a breath of air. He went back to the dining room and told them it was all set. Mrs. Smith clapped her hands together, as she was prone to do when pleased or excited about something. "That's fine, Mark. Now don't you worry, we'll have everything ready for her." She had called him by his first name again! Not that he objected.

When he left to get ready for church, Gail walked out to the porch with him. Crossing her arms, she said, "So we are special friends, huh?" He then realized that she and her mother had probably heard the entire conversation, at least his part of it. "Yes," he replied, "I think that's an adequate description." She playfully punched him on the arm. Pretending to be hurt, he said, "Ouch! You are attacking your pastor." With mock horror, she replied, "Oh, Reverend Thomas, please forgive me." And they both broke out laughing. "It's been a really good day," he said. "See you tonight."

On the short drive back home, he realized that he was *and deeply* in love. He just hoped Gail felt the same way.

As he was talking with several members after the service ended, Gail approached him and said, "Reverend Thomas, we need to schedule rehearsal for the children's choir and their part in the Christmas music program." There was no sign of the playfulness she had exhibited earlier but there was a definite look of humor in her eyes. Trying his best to act serious, he suggested they talk about it on Monday.

Chapter 11

During the week Mark ate breakfast at home so he could use the morning hours for study and sermon preparation, but on Saturday he would go to the restaurant and have the special. It was Saturday, December 12, and he was thinking about the schedule for the next two weeks—the church Christmas program, Christmas parties he had been invited to, and, of course, his mother's visit.

Stump Harris came in, pulled out a chair and sat down, asking Myrtle for coffee. As he lit another cigarette, Stump said, "Haven't seen you much lately." Taking a sip of coffee, Mark replied, "It's been busy." Stump grinned and said, "So I've noticed." When Mark gave him a questioning look, the farmer/policeman said, "Just joking preacher. Gail's a fine girl. Comes from a fine family."

"What was her father like?" Mark asked. Taking a sip of his coffee, Stump replied, "Salt of the earth. Honest, dependable, and a loyal friend. As we said in the Army, he was a man you wouldn't mind sharing a foxhole with." Mark guessed that was the highest compliment Stump could give anyone. "She'll be a good wife." That remark made Mark choke on his sip of coffee. "Stump! We have only dated for a couple of months. Aren't you taking things a little too far?" Inhaling his cigarette, Stump grinned and said, "Preacher, some things are just meant to be."

Bending closer, he asked, "Have you picked up any clues about Sammy Garber's death?" Mark nodded no. Stump leaned back in his chair and stared at the ceiling. "Me neither. Some days I wonder if we will ever solve the puzzle, ever know what happened." It was clear that in time, others may forget Sammy Garber's death. Not Stump Harris. He would do his best to solve the puzzle as he put it.

On the ride to Valdosta, Mark told Gail about the two words Sammy spoke. "There may have been a third word that he could not clearly enunciate., but I know he spoke 'ran' and 'Joseph'. Do you have any idea what he may have meant?" She thought for a moment and then shook her head. "No and it doesn't make sense. I know most everyone in Gentry and there's no one who is called Joseph." He shared with her about the attempts to find out what the words may have meant and what they had to do with Sammy's death.

"We visited the Kelly family the following week, but they couldn't shed any light on what happened. Stump thought that Sammy may have been at the Kelly house since that's the direction he came from, but they couldn't help. Sue was in Valdosta with cousins, Doyle was working, and Wanda said he didn't come to the house." An expression came over Gail's face that he had not seen before. It was a look of contempt. She spoke and said, "If you can believe Wanda Kelly."

"Why would you say that? What's wrong with Wanda Kelly?" Gail bit her lip as if she had already said too much. "Okay. As Daddy used to say, the horse is out of the barn. Mark, it's not so much what I know about Wanda Kelly as what I feel about her. Do you know about 'women's intuition'?" He nodded as if he did, curious as to where this was headed. "Let me back up," she said. "Doyle's first wife, Clara, died of cancer when Sue was six. He met Wanda in a restaurant in Valdosta where she worked as a waitress. Doyle must have been lonely, and Wanda wanted someone to marry. They only knew one another about six weeks when they married. Wanda was eighteen and Doyle was twenty-nine. That was ten years ago, so Wanda is now twenty-eight and Doyle is thirty-nine. I guess some men would find her attractive, or maybe I should say, appealing. Some may say she has sex appeal. She's nice looking with a nice figure and has an alluring demeanor."

"But that doesn't make her untrustworthy," he interjected. "But how she acts does," Gail said. "The first couple of years they were married, everything seemed okay. Then Wanda started flirting with younger men. Men more her age. Wanda Kelly doesn't act like a married woman and Doyle must either be blind or chooses to ignore her flirtations. I wouldn't trust her if she told me Christmas was in thirteen days!" Her level of disapproval was rising as well as the intensity of her words. "And she isn't much of a mother to Sue. I've had Sue in my classes. Wanda never attends any school functions and does nothing to be supportive of Sue. In my opinion, she falls far short when it comes to being a good wife and mother." With that she stopped talking but clamped her lips tightly, crossed her arms and stared ahead.

Mark drove for a couple of miles and then said, "Well, we don't want to let that horse out of the barn again." It took a moment for her to laugh. He let another mile go by and said, "Gail, I saw a side of you tonight I had not seen." With a toss of her head, she replied, "I told you when you ate with us that there's a lot you don't know about me." *But I hope to learn more*, he thought. Then he counted back the weeks to that first date. Only five weeks! They had come a long way in a short period of time.

They resumed talking about Christmas and a thought froze him. *He had to buy her a present!* He hadn't bought a girl a Christmas present since his senior year in high school and that was a Whitman's Sampler. He would have to do better than that this time. Much better!

As they came to the outskirts of Valdosta, he said, "Gail, would you mind if we skipped the movie and did some shopping? Since mother is coming for Christmas, I need to get her a present. Maybe you can help?" She thought it would be a wonderful idea to shop. Parking the car on Patterson street, they held hands and leisurely strolled past the stores, stopping to look at the window displays and admire the Christmas decorations. Passing one of the women's clothing stores, Gail said, "Oh, look at that!" The window had three mannequins, so he wasn't sure what she was looking at."

"What am I supposed to look at?"

"That blue sweater," she said. "Isn't it gorgeous?" The sweater was a light blue and Mark could only guess about the material. He made a mental note and they continued to walk and look. They walked four blocks of Patterson Street, looking on both sides of the street and then did the same on Ashley Street. Although she commented on several other things, she did not show the same enthusiasm as she did for the sweater. She did make several suggestions for a gift for his mother.

When they entered Belk-Hudson, he reminded her that this was the site of their first encounter. He laughed and said, "When you finished shopping and left that night, I didn't think I would ever see you again. And now, here we are, just one year later." At that moment his former manager called out his name and came over, greeting Mark warmly. "Ready to come back to work? It's getting really busy and I could use some good help," he said. "Thanks, but I've found my calling," Mark replied. He then introduced Gail to the manager. As he shook her hand, the manager told her she had found a good man. With a serious look, she replied, "Yes, I'm learning that."

After walking and window shopping for two hours, they went on to Shoney's for their customary meal—burger, fries, coke, and strawberry pie. On the ride home, Gail wanted to know more about his mother. "You will like her," he said. She replied, "I have no doubt I will."

Mark was already thinking ahead to next week and when he could return to Valdosta to purchase a certain blue sweater.

~

If no one invited Mark for Sunday dinner, he would eat with Gail and her mother. On this Sunday, he was hoping no one would invite him because he needed to ask Mrs. Smith Gail's sweater size. He was almost disappointed when Harley and Jeanette Bass asked him to eat with them.

After the meal, Jeanette said she would make some coffee to go with their dessert and the two men moved to the living room. Mark had learned that Harley and Jeanette were people he could confide in. He had consulted Harley about some sensitive issues in the church and always received good advice. Deciding to take a chance he said, "Harley, tell me about the Kelly family." Harley gave him a quizzical look and asked, "Anything in particular?"

Shifting in his chair, Mark continued. "Just curious. Next to Mrs. Garber, they would have been the most affected by Sammy's death what with him dating Sue." Mark felt a twinge of guilt as he was attempting to guide Harley to the real point of the conversation. Was he being deceitful? Harley then related the same basic information that Gail had: the death of Doyle's first wife and the brief romance with Wanda that resulted in the marriage. He omitted any mention of Wanda's flirtatious behavior but that was his nature. Harley didn't gossip about people.

Jeanette came from the kitchen and sat on the couch with Harley. "What are we talking about?" she asked. Harley replied, "He wants to know about the Kelly's." The look they exchanged told Mark there was more they could say—if they would. Looking at them he said, "I respect the both of you and value your opinion. I'm not trying to pull skeletons out of a closet or dig up juicy gossip. It's just...well, I'm still bothered by the whole ordeal of Sammy's death and am trying to help those who are hurting because of it." At least that's partly the truth he thought, and he was certainly one of those still hurting.

Jeanette was the one who spoke. "Preacher, I wouldn't want this to go out of this house, even though lots of folks in Gentry know it." He nodded that he understood and agreed. She continued. "When Clara died--that was Sue's mama--Doyle was at a loss. He was lonely, and he had a six-year-old daughter to raise. I think Wanda was just looking for some man to take care of her. That's my opinion but I think it's true or I wouldn't say it. Anyway, they got married. I think that after a while, the new wore off, so to speak, for Wanda. Gentry cannot compare with Valdosta with stores and things to do. I think she was eighteen or nineteen, and she had to take on the responsibility of being a wife and mother to a child that wasn't hers. Wanda seems to be the kind of woman who likes excitement and Doyle Kelly is a good man but far from being exciting. He's a hard worker and good provider but doesn't do much socially. Anyway, it seems that after the first year, Wanda started acting differently, flirting with men her age, even accepting rides with men to go to Tadlock or Valdosta. And she stopped going to church with Doyle and Sue."

Harley lifted a hand to stop Jeanette and asked, "Preacher, what does this have to do with Sammy's death? While Wanda's behavior is, what's the word—deplorable—I don't see how it has any bearing on his death."

Mark leaned forward, thoughtfully rubbing his hands together. "You are probably right, and I apologize for even involving y'all in this conversation." He paused and continued. "The way he died and my part in it has left so many unanswered questions." With a gentle voice, Harley said, "Preacher, don't take offense, but maybe 'these questions' as you call them, aren't valid. Maybe they are your way of dealing with Sammy's death. You got pulled into the whole thing and I'm sure it was a little traumatic." Mark saw this as a gracious way to end the conversation, so he nodded his assent.

Jeanette stood and returned to the kitchen and announced that dessert was being served. As he left, he thanked them for the meal as well as the opportunity to unburden himself. "Anytime," Harley said, and Mark knew he meant it.

At church that night, he was able to discreetly ask Mrs.

Smith what size sweater he should buy for Gail. "No telling now," he said. She smiled and winked. After church, Gail told him she wouldn't be able to meet the next day. "We have something at school and besides, there really isn't any church business that can't wait." For once, Mark was not disappointed at missing an opportunity to be with her. It meant he could go to Valdosta and purchase her Christmas present.

Entering the store, a clerk asked if she could help him. He asked for the blue sweater in the window in Gail's size. The clerk brought it and asked if he wanted it gift wrapped, which he did. When she told him the price, he had to refrain from asking if she was sure. He knew he could probably buy a similar sweater at Belk-Hudson for half the cost of this one. *But this was the sweater Gail liked.* After paying for the sweater, he decided to shop for his mother and perhaps something for Mrs. Smith. He put the sweater in his car and was crossing the street when a car passed. He could have sworn that was Wanda Kelly, but it wasn't the Kelly car and the driver wasn't Doyle! Maybe he was mistaken but if it was Wanda, this added credence to what Gail and Jeanette had said about her. If it was her, she was brazen in her behavior.

Clothes were out of the question for his mother and Mrs. Smith, so he spent the next two hours going from store to store looking for gifts. Buying that Whitman's Sampler for that girl in high school was much easier. He wondered what happened to her. He saw her once when he returned home after completing basic training. They had dated most of their senior year in school. Her main objective after graduation was to marry and start a family. He had other plans, so they broke up the week after graduation. It was the first time he had thought about her in years. He would have to ask his mother what happened to her.

He finally purchased gifts, hoping he had made the correct choices and returned to Gentry in time for supper with Mrs. Cole. She told him Gail had called to remind him of the children's choir rehearsal after church on Wednesday. Next Sunday night was the Christmas program. Where was December going? And his mother would be here next week!

He went to bed feeling both pleased and excited. Pleased that he had purchased the sweater Gail liked and excited about next week and his mother's visit. Could his life get any better? About two o'clock, he had the nightmare. He awoke, shaking as usual, and sat up on the side of the bed, wondering if he would always be tormented in this way. An hour passed before he fell asleep again.

Jimmy Deas

Chapter 12

The Wednesday night service at the Gentry Baptist Church consisted of the adults meeting in the sanctuary for prayer and Bible study. The children and teenagers met in mission study groups. All activities were shortened on the Wednesday before Christmas for a final rehearsal of the Christmas program. Since he had never participated in a Christmas program as a pastor, he chose to observe and learn, which mostly meant staying out of the way.

He would read the gospel accounts of the birth of Jesus Christ, the adult choir would sing hymns, and the children's choir, dressed in Biblical costume, would enter at the appropriate time as the characters in the Christmas story. It was a madhouse as the adults fitted the children in costumes which were bath robes and pieces of cloth wrapped around their heads. Mark was impressed with the wise men's crowns, made of cardboard and painted gold, and the angel costumes which were a little more elaborate.

To get out of the temporary chaos, he walked down to the room that served as storage for literature and where the Sunday School secretary tabulated class reports. He decided to use paper clips to mark the pages in his Bible with the scriptures he would read in order to avoid fumbling for the correct page. As he turned, he knocked a box of pencils off the desk. Some had rolled under the desk, forcing him to get on his hands and knees to retrieve them. Hearing a giggle, he stood and saw Gail behind him. "It blesses my heart to see our pastor down on his knees," she said jokingly. "Well," he replied with an air of spiritual superiority, "Some of my flock need serious prayer."

"I need some safety pins," she said and stepped toward the desk. She slipped on one of the pencils and would have fallen if he had not caught her. He held her for a moment and then drew her close and softly kissed her. Lifting his head, he said, "I love you." In a low whisper, she replied, "I love you too." There might have been a second kiss but for a child's voice down the hallway calling for Miz Gail.

Mark had never known such elation in his life. *She loved him!* He wanted to revel in the moment but heard someone calling for him. He found it difficult to focus on his part, constantly glancing at her as she helped direct the entry of the children.

After two practices, the leaders pronounced it satisfactory and everyone started for home. Mark would be the last to leave since he had to turn off the lights and heat and lock the doors. Gail lingered, taking her time putting up the costumes. She waited on the front stoop as he locked the door. They stood and looked at one another in the light from the streetlamps. She broke the silence. "Mark, are you sure?"

"Gail, I've never been surer of anything in my life except for the fact that Jesus died for my sins. Are you sure?"

"Mark, this may sound funny, but I feel we've been headed to this moment since you came here. It was inevitable."

"Then why were you so distant at first?" Without hesitation, she replied, "Because I wanted to be sure that you were the husband God wanted for me. Remember, I told you about the disappointing romance in college and I never wanted that to happen again. I had put my life in God's hands and only wanted the man of his choosing."

She smiled and asked, "Why did it take you so long to ask me for a date? I was beginning to think you never would." *Now that was a revelation to him!* "For the same reasons. I wanted to know and follow God's will and not let my personal desires or impulses get in the way."

There was a silence and they kissed again. "I'll see you

Saturday," he said. Her answer surprised him. "How about coming out for lunch tomorrow? School's out for Christmas so I'm free." "I would love it," he said, and kissed her again. As she turned to leave, she looked over her shoulder and playfully said, "You are way ahead of your father." It took him a minute to realize what she meant. As she drove away, he muttered, "I guess I am."

She met him on the porch the next day and lifted her head for a kiss before they went inside. During the meal, Mrs. Smith kept looking at them both with a twinkle in her eye. She knows, Mark said to himself. *How do mothers always know?* After cleaning off the table, Gail asked if he had to go. "Not really. My sermon is ready, and I'm caught up with my visitation." She suggested they take a walk around the farm. It wasn't cold but cool enough to wear a jacket and it was a gorgeous day without a cloud in the sky. As they walked, she put her arm in his. They didn't know Mrs. Smith was watching from the window with a smile on her face and a "thank-you" prayer in her heart.

"Mark," Gail said, "we have lots to talk about."

"Okay. But do we have to do it all in one afternoon?" She laughed that laugh he had come to love and wanted to hear for the rest of his life. "No," she replied, "I guess we can take our time." So they walked around the farm holding hands, occasionally stopping to kiss; and sometimes he would just silently hold her, and she would lean her head against his chest.

The conversation ranged from serious to humorous and from the past to the future. "Do you really think it's possible you waved at me when we passed through Bishop?" He shrugged. "Maybe, I always waved at the pretty girls." She playfully punched him on the shoulder. "I will confess something. When you made your purchase at Belk-Hudson last Christmas, I was hoping you would pay by check, so I could ask for some identification and see where you lived." She punched him again. "You are a rascal." He told her about Bill Swain and the challenge to ask her for a date. Shaking her head, she said, "I can't believe you men!"

Later, she asked if he had ever been serious about someone. "Just the puppy-love crush I had in high school. All of the years I was in the Air Force and at college, I dated but it was never serious; and none lasted long." She stopped, turned, and looked him in the face. "Mark, what makes you feel I'm that special person? I mean, how do you know you love me?"

Placing his hands on her shoulders, he said, "Gail, my dad gave me just one piece of advice about love and marriage. He told me never to date someone that wasn't a Christian and not to marry until I found the woman I wanted to spend the rest of my life with. You are both of those. And I just couldn't help loving you." She leaned her head against his chest and said, "That's all I need to know."

It was late in the day when they returned to the house. When they walked in, Mark smelled the aroma of food cooking and panic seized him. "Oh, no! I forgot about supper with Mrs. Cole." Mrs. Smith held up her hand and said, "Don't worry. I called Edith and told her you wouldn't make it tonight." Mark breathed a sigh of relief. She continued, "Wash up, supper's almost ready." Being a discreet woman, Mrs. Smith didn't ask questions. The look on Gail's face told her all she needed to know. While they were eating, Mark thought back to the day in October when he came for lunch and they discussed the dissension Stella Boyd was causing. At the time, he wasn't sure he would last out the month. He remembered how calm and encouraging Mrs. Smith had been that day and how she had spoken up for him at church. Now here he was, still the pastor of Gentry Baptist Church; in love with her daughter and, God willing, she would be his mother-in-law.

~

It was the Sunday before Christmas and the worship attendance was noticeably larger. The adult choir and children's choir combined to sing a song that was part of the program that night. A chorus of "Amen" rose from the congregation when the song ended. Mark was excited as he moved to the pulpit to preach. Using the scriptures about the birth of the Savior, he emphasized that:

(1)Man could not get to God, so God came to man.

(2)The greatest Christmas present is salvation.

(3)Man's greatest response to God is worship.

As the choir took their seats before the worship service started, Gail leaned up and whispered, "You are eating with us today." After church, two families extended invitations, but he answered that someone had already invited him. Driving to Gail's house, he wondered how long it would be before the congregation learned of their romance. In Gentry, it wouldn't take long for everyone to know.

As far as Mark was concerned, no one could cook like his mother. Living on a farm provided fresh vegetables in summer and canned ones in the winter. They had peach and apple trees and the fruit was used to make many cobblers and pies. But Mrs. Smith would run his mother a close race. The more he ate at her table, the more he enjoyed her cooking; and second helpings were hard to refuse. If this kept up, he may have to buy a new suit—with a size larger waist!

Gail had to return to church early to prepare for the Christmas program so the visiting time was shortened. Gail gave him a quick kiss and left. As he was about to leave, Mrs. Smith asked if he would wait a minute. Wondering what she wanted, he sat down on the edge of a chair. Taking the chair opposite, she said, "Mark, Gail and I had a talk last night. I just want you to know how happy I am for you and Gail. From the day she was born, I prayed that God would bring her the right man. I believe that you are the answer to that prayer and as far as I'm concerned, you are already a part of this family." A lump formed in his throat, preventing him from speaking for a minute. He finally cleared his throat and thanked her for sharing that with him. He told her about the advice his father had given him, and that Gail was the person he wanted to spend the rest of his life with. "Mark, your father was a very wise man and he gave you some excellent advice." Standing to go, he impulsively hugged her. With a smile she said, "You're going to fit in well."

The Christmas program was well attended. Mark had encouraged the members to invite their family, friends, and neighbors. Except for a wise man losing his crown and a shepherd who accidentally hit another one with his staff, the program went as planned. Mark closed with a few remarks about the significance of Christmas, invited everyone to the fellowship that would follow, and was prepared to pray when Harley Bass interrupted him. "Just a minute preacher.

There's one more thing we need to do," as he walked up to the pulpit. Mark was puzzled. What did he forget?

Harley said, "Folks, Brother Mark has only been our preacher for seven months, but we have come to love him. He has made a difference in our church in many ways and we want to show our appreciation." With that said, he reached inside his coat and removed an envelope. "Preacher, this is for you. Merry Christmas from your congregation." Taking the envelope, he lifted the flap and saw a $100 bill. He sucked in his breath. This was so unexpected. He stammered out a heartfelt thank you and said he was truly at a loss for words. With a big grin, Harley said, "Now we know how much it takes to get him not to talk." This was followed by good natured laughter from the congregation. Harley then held up a hand for silence and said, "Let's let him pray so we can go eat."

Following the fellowship, he walked Gail to her car but refrained from kissing her due to the presence of others in the parking area. She smiled and said, "See you for lunch tomorrow?" He grinned and replied, "You better believe it."

Later, while undressing, he removed the envelope from his shirt pocket and stared at the crisp bill. Tears filled his eyes as he thought about the generosity of his congregation and he felt so undeserving. He thanked God for bringing these people into his life.

~

Monday morning he was up early, ate breakfast and started preparing his sermons for the next Sunday. His scripture was Luke 2:20, *"And the shepherds returned, glorifying and praising God for all the things that they had heard and seen, as it was told unto them."* After their encounter with the Christ child, the shepherds had to return to their homes and occupations and the routine of life. However, they continued to praise God for their experience. He wanted to emphasize that after Christmas people returned to work, to school, to the routine of life; but, like the shepherds, they needed to continue to praise God.

Glancing at his watch, he saw that it was 10:15. Laying down his pen, he thought about his mother's visit. He had not seen her since March when the college had spring break. Many students opted for the beach and headed for Florida. Mark had gone to Athens to visit his mother and Aunt Catherine. The combination of military and college had limited his visits home. His anticipation of her visit was growing. Let's see. It took him about him five to six hours to drive from Valdosta to Athens. It should take her about seven hours, with stops for lunch, gas, and restroom. He calculated she should arrive about four o'clock.

He resumed reading and making notes, but it was

difficult to focus, and he kept glancing at his watch. Laughing at himself, he realized he was more focused on lunch with Gail than he was with the shepherds. Laying down the pen again, he reflected on how blessed he was and how special this Christmas promised to be. He then thought of those for whom Christmas would be difficult, such as Nell Garber and Sue Kelly. And how many more in Gentry would find it difficult to rejoice? Like Howard Fry who would spend Christmas day with Tilly although she could no longer remember the joy and fun. Bowing his head, he prayed for them--praying that the heavenly Father would bless them in a special way during the Christmas season.

As he read more of his commentary, it occurred to him that in some way's things weren't that different in people's lives in the twentieth century than in the first century. People still lived with fear, anxiety, oppression, illness, death, and uncertainty. *The first Christmas did not eliminate all of man's problems; it brought hope and the power to overcome all of man's problems!*

At 11:30, Mark ended his study and drove to Gail's. She informed him that after lunch, they were going to Tadlock to purchase the needed groceries for the Christmas meal. After a lunch of homemade soup, cornbread, and Jell-O salad, they drove to Tadlock, in Mrs. Smith's Impala.

As they entered the store, he saw Dr. Riley Barber, pastor

of the First Baptist Church of Tadlock. They had met at an associational meeting and he occasionally saw Barber when visiting the hospital in Tadlock. He was in his mid-fifties, with a great personality, and quick smile. The kind of person who made anyone feel accepted. Seeing Mark approach, he spoke first. "Hi Mark. How are things in Gentry?" He replied, "Going well Dr. Barber. It's a learning experience."

"Please, please, call me Riley." That would be difficult for Mark to do. His parents had raised him to be polite and courteous to anyone older than him. If he used some older person's first name, it was always preceded with a Mr. or Mrs. Barber continued, "All churches are learning experiences. After thirty years and four churches, I'm still learning."

"You graduated from seminary?" Mark asked. "Yes, I did. New Orleans. Why do you ask?" Mark then briefly shared his desire to attend seminary. "Could I come and talk with you after Christmas?" With his ready smile, the other pastor said to give him a call. "Buying for your Christmas dinner?" he inquired. Nodding towards Gail and her mother, he replied, "No, just rode down with some church members." Boy, he thought, that sounded stupid. Looking at the Smith's, Barber said, "Oh, yes, Gail Smith. Beautiful voice. She sang at our revival last spring. Good to see you Mark. I better get home before Gladys sends the police for me." They wished each other a Merry Christmas and Barber headed to the cashier line. As Mark rejoined the women, Mrs. Smith asked if his mother had any likes or dislikes about food. "Not that I know of," he replied. "Okay," she said, "I'll fix like I normally do."

Mrs. Smith filled one cart and asked Mark to get another one. He wondered how four people would be able to eat all she was buying. He later learned that she prepared a complete Christmas dinner for one of the poorer families in Gentry. They returned home, and she told Gail and Mark to go for a walk while she cooked supper. Protesting for just a minute, Gail acquiesced and led him out the door. For the next hour, they shared their dreams and hopes for the future. He told her about his conversation with Riley Barber. She got noticeably quieter and didn't talk as much on the return to the house.

As much as he wanted to stay and visit, Mark excused himself and left after supper, explaining about his desire to finish his sermons so he could enjoy his mother's visit and Christmas. It was almost midnight when he finished his notes. He lay in bed, excited about seeing his mother the next day and hoping she would like Gail. But why wouldn't she like Gail? He fell asleep and hardly moved until 6:30 Tuesday morning.

Jimmy Deas

Chapter 13

Mark awoke with a start at 6:15, got up, put on the coffee, and headed for the shower. At 7:00 he resumed his preparation. Mark always prayed for guidance and understanding before he studied. This morning he added a prayer for travel safety for his mother. Four hours, he thought. He should be finished in four hours. At 11:15, he finished. Time to gas up his car before heading to Gail's.

Arriving at the Smith house, he could tell they were excited about his mother's arrival also. He had given her directions to Gail's house just in case something came up and he wasn't at home. Preacher's schedules and plans could change quickly. Fortunately, no one really needed him that afternoon. School was out for Christmas and most people were doing their final preparations for the holidays.

Mark had only seen part of the house--living room,

dining room, kitchen, and one of the bathrooms. Gail led him down the hallway to the room his mother would use. It was just as he expected. Everything was neat and functional, and everything matched. She closed the door and raised her head for a kiss. Putting her arms around him, she said, "Oh, Mark, I hope she likes me." He moved her back to arm's length and said, "Gail, trust me, my mother will love you." Laying her head on his chest, she murmured, "I hope so." A call from her mother brought them out of the bedroom. She needed Mark to open a jar lid that was stuck. After he got it open, she smiled and said how nice it was to have a man around the house. Gail rolled her eyes.

As the time approached 4:00, Mark was beginning to worry. Had there been a problem? A flat tire? Had she missed a turn somewhere? By his calculations, she should have arrived by now. Then he heard the car coming up the drive and breathed a sigh of relief. Mrs. Smith was wiping her hands on her apron and smiling. Gail smiled, but Mark could tell she was nervous. He went out to greet his mother. Wrapping his arms around her, he held her for a minute before speaking. "Mom, I'm so glad you came and I'm glad you're safe." She smiled and asked, "You didn't worry about me did you, son?" He replied, "No more than you worried about me when I was growing up."

Hearing Gail and Mrs. Smith coming down the steps,

he took her arm and walked towards them. "Mom, this is Gail." Gail hugged her warmly and told her how glad she was to meet her. Mrs. Smith stepped forward, took her hand, and said, "I'm Rebecca and we are so delighted that you have come to visit Mark and stay with us." His mother responded, "Call me Ruth." Mrs. Smith took her by the arm and said, "I know you've had a long day. Why don't you come inside and freshen up while the kids get your luggage?" As they walked up the steps together, Gail said, "They act like old friends, don't they?" Mark didn't say anything, but he was pleased.

After supper, they talked and laughed until 10:00. Mark saw his mother stifle a yawn and Mrs. Smith saw it too. "Ruth, I know you must be tired. Let me show you your room." They all stood, and Mark hugged his mother goodnight. She placed a hand on each side of his face and pulled it forward, so she could kiss him on the forehead. He said goodnight and started to leave. Gail followed him to the porch where she said, "Oh Mark, I just love her." Mark said, "Gail, I can tell you she loves you too." He kissed her goodnight and went home.

The next morning, he went to Gail's for breakfast. His mother was acting more like a member of the family than a guest. She was setting the table when he arrived. He asked if she had slept well and she said she had. "It's so peaceful and quiet here, just like when we lived on the farm. I don't mind living in Athens, but it can be noisy at times. "

After breakfast he told his mother he wanted to introduce her to some of the people in Gentry. He asked Gail if she wanted to go but she declined, saying she needed to do some laundry. As they pulled out of the drive, his mother said, "Mark, I can see why you are in love with Gail. She is one of the sweetest people I have ever met."

"I'm glad you like her mom."

"Son let me ask. Are there any wedding plans?"

"No mom. All of this has happened so quickly. We've only been dating for two months. I want to wait for the right time." Grinning, he said, "And besides, I haven't had any practice asking a girl to marry me." They exchanged a laugh.

Pointing to the Cole house, he told her that's where he lived, and they would stop by on the way back. Parking in front of the post office, they went in and he introduced her to Edith Cole. "Mom, this is my landlady and she has been like a second mother here in Gentry." His mother extended her hand. "So pleased to meet you. Mark has told me so much about you in his letters." Edith Cole, responded with, "He has been a joy to have as a renter and a blessing as a pastor." They chatted for a few minutes and then excused themselves and he went to Tuttle's Grocery where he introduced her to Bob and Marion. Next they crossed the street to the restaurant. "Myrtle, I want you to meet my mother." Seeing the look of disapproval on her face, he quickly said, "Now mom, I called her Mrs. Myrtle once and she threatened to hit me with a frying pan if I called her that again." Myrtle laughed and said, "That's right." She extended her hand. "It's plain Myrtle. Myrtle Johns and it's a pleasure to meet you Mrs. Thomas. We think a lot of your son. He's done some good things in Gentry."

They chatted for a few minutes and as they left, she said, "Don't bother coming on Saturday for breakfast." When he asked why, she told him they were closing at noon on Thursday to go see the grandchildren in Panama City. "Good for you. Be careful and I'll see you when you get back." As they returned to the car, he saw Nell Garber coming out of the post office and introduced his mother to her. "Mrs. Thomas, I can't tell you how much your son has helped me through a difficult time." Her lip began to tremble. "I'll let him tell you about it. How long will you be visiting in Gentry?" When told a week, she replied, "Then maybe I'll see you in church Sunday."

Mark drove back to the apartment. After she looked around his apartment, they sat in the easy chairs and he told her about Sammy Garber's death. "Now I see why she wears grief like she does," she said. He was puzzled. "What do you mean, 'she wears grief'?", he asked. "Oh son, she wears it like a dress or a coat. It may not be obvious to everyone, but I could see it right off."

"Mom, the puzzling thing is, no one knows why Sammy ran out in front of that car or who or what he was running from. The local policeman and I have done our best to solve the mystery." Giving him an inquiring look, she said, "I thought I raised a preacher, not a detective." He laughed. "You did. It's just that I was such a part of Sammy's death and I feel there's got to be an explanation." He started to tell her about the nightmares but decided not to, not wanting her to worry about him.

They returned to the Smith's for lunch and spent the afternoon trading stories about the families. One thing that seemed to connect the two mothers was that they were widows. They had experienced the sorrow of losing their mate. Gail asked his mother to tell about Mark as a kid. She related some of the funnier things he did that made all of them laugh. Mrs. Smith asked if he really stood on the sidewalk in Bishop and waved at the tourists passing through town. "Lord, yes," she replied. "That was a favorite pastime of all the boys in Bishop." His mother told stories--true stories--that Mark hoped had long been forgotten, including some that resulted in punishment inflicted on the backside of his body. After one laughing spell, she got serious and said, "One thing I can say about Mark. He was a boy and may have been mischievous at times, but he never did anything mean or that would hurt someone else."

The storytelling was ended by the need to eat an early supper in order to get to church.

The Wednesday night worship format was simple: two hymns (Christmas carols on this night), and a prayer time, followed by a Bible study. On this night, Mark announced a change, telling the attendees they were going to participate in the service. He read Matthew's account of the wise men bringing gifts to Jesus. "Now, I am asking each of you to tell us briefly what the most special gift was you received for Christmas and why it made you feel special. I'll start." He told of the BB gun he received when he was eight and how he imagined he was a big game hunter in Africa or an Indian fighter in the west. People responded eagerly although at one point he had to remind them to be brief. He was surprised when his mother stood since she was a visitor in a room of mostly strangers. Looking at Mark, she said, "The first Christmas gift you gave me." She sat down without elaborating. He remembered that gift! He was five years old, had saved his change, and his dad drove to Watkinsville to the Five and Ten Cent Store. The gift was a delicate handkerchief with crocheted edge in lavender or rose-colored thread. He couldn't be sure.

Then he said they would share how long that gift lasted.

The point he wanted to make was that the gifts people give and receive usually don't last long. They wear out, tear up, and are thrown away. The only lasting gift is the one God gives--salvation through Jesus Christ. Again, he went first. The BB gun lasted three years. Playing one day, he grasped it by the barrel and swung it at an imaginary foe. He swung too hard, hit a tree, and broke the gun. The people responded with answers ranging from a few months to several years at most. The people were illustrating his point. When it was his mother's turn she stood and said," I still have it." He couldn't believe it! That handkerchief was twenty years old! It should have worn out years ago. *She still had it!* A lump formed in his throat and he was glad he could just motion for the next person to share and he didn't have to say anything.

~

Mark arose on Christmas morning, made coffee, had his morning Bible reading and prayer, and took his time getting dressed. The women had decided to have a late breakfast on Christmas morning and eat the big meal in the afternoon. He couldn't remember when he had anticipated Christmas this much. He was pulling out of the yard when he remembered the presents. Arriving at the house shortly before 9:00, Gail greeted him at the door with a kiss. "Where's Mom?" Gail nodded over her shoulder. "In the kitchen with mother. Mark, it's amazing how fast they have become friends." With a knowing smile, he said, "That's because they have something in common." Tossing her head, she said, "You think so?"

Entering the kitchen, he saw his mother stirring a bowl of batter. "Is that what I think it is," he asked. She turned and with a pleased look said, "Buttermilk pancakes. Rebecca asked what you liked for breakfast and when I said buttermilk pancakes, she suggested I make some." *Buttermilk pancakes!* Christmas was off to a good start.

After a leisurely breakfast, they moved to the living room to share their gifts. Knowing her fondness for scarves, Mark gave his mother a colorful scarf, a unique brooch, and a recording of George Beverly Shea singing gospel songs. Remembering that Mrs. Smith had recently broken her favorite serving bowl, he gave her an almost identical one. The women seemed pleased with his selections of gifts. Acting on Mark's advice, Gail gave his mother a scarf and a pair of gloves. Gail handed her mother the largest present under the tree. It was an all-weather coat with zip-out lining. "Oh, Gail," she protested, "I didn't need this. I have a coat." With a forceful tone of voice Gail replied, "Mother, that coat should have been replaced five years ago." Whereupon her mother smiled and thanked her.

Mark then handed Gail her present and anxiously

waited to see her response. When she opened it, she squealed, pressed it to her chest and said, "Oh, Mark, you shouldn't have!" The look on her face and the sound of her voice made him want to go buy her a dozen more. She then handed him his present. The small box was heavy for its size. Holding it to his ear, he shook it. "Mark Thomas, quit fooling around and open it." Tearing the paper away, he could see it was a box containing a Bible. Removing the lid, he saw a black, genuine leather Bible with Rev. Mark Thomas embossed across the bottom. "Do you like it?" He nodded. "It's perfect."

They refilled their coffee cups and started talking about past Christmases. Suddenly, Mrs. Smith got up and went to her bedroom, returning with two boxes. Gail protested, "Oh no. Not the pictures." The boxes were opened, and the photos passed around along with the matching story. They laughed, Gail and her mother reminisced over the photos, and in the process, Mark felt he was getting to know Gail better. At least more about her. Gail said. "Mrs. Thomas, next time you come, bring some pictures of Mark when he was little." *Next time! They acted as if it was already planned.*

The phone rang. It was Robert, calling from Tallahassee to wish them Merry Christmas. Each of the kids and his wife took the phone to talk with her. Then Robert took the phone and in response to a question, Mrs. Smith answered, "No. No announcement yet. Maybe soon." Mark felt his face start to color. *What's wrong with these usually sensible people?* He and Gail had only dated for two months.

At three o'clock, they ate their Christmas meal. At his mother's suggestion, they all joined hands for the blessing. As he prayed, he especially thanked their heavenly Father for a memorable Christmas with loved ones. As he said, "Amen", Gail gave his hand an affectionate squeeze.

The days passed quickly, and it was time for his mother to leave, although Gail and her mother tried to get her to stay longer. On Monday night, they ate and talked until 10:00, all agreeing that was late enough and his mother needed a good night's rest. She wanted to leave early, so Mark went to the Smith's for an early breakfast, so she could leave by 8:00. With all the good-byes, it was almost 8:30 before she drove away. The hug between the two older women indicated the bond of affection that had developed between them. Mrs. Smith said, "You call here and let us know when you get home." Mark and Gail stood arm in arm, watching her leave. She said, "Mark, I really love your mother, she's so sweet."

"Gail, she loves you too." When she asked how he knew, he simply responded, "She told me so."

Chapter 14

January was unusually cold in North Florida. For eight consecutive days, the daily temperatures did not reach 60 degrees with a hard freeze at night. When outside, Mark had to wear a sweater under his jacket to stay warm.

It was during the cold spell that he visited the Fry's and was concerned by what he saw. Howard's arthritis was worse, and it was difficult for him to take care of Tilly. She lay in the bed not moving except to periodically lick her lips. He was concerned that they were not eating sufficiently. Their two sons had suggested a nursing home but Howard, a proud and stubborn man, refused to consider the idea. Neighbors had offered to help with the cooking, housework, and taking care of Tilly; but he refused their offers. Walking to his car, he considered contacting the sons but was reluctant. He didn't like to interfere in other people's business, a trait he inherited from his parents. He would wait a couple of days and check on them again. Driving away, he reflected that Howard wasn't the only person who needed help of some kind but due to pride, stubbornness, or both, failed to get help. The alcoholic, the liar, the thief...an almost endless list of struggling, suffering people who refused the very help they needed. And, he sadly thought, the worst form of this refusal is the sinner who refuses to acknowledge his sin and accept God's offer of salvation through faith in Jesus Christ.

He was having Saturday breakfast at the restaurant when Stump Harris came in, ordered coffee, and sat down across the table. "Preacher, looks like we're going to close the book on Sammy Garber." When asked why, he replied, "It's been four months and we haven't discovered anything new about his death. I talked to the sheriff this week. The deputy that investigated and the Highway Patrol wrote it up as an accident. Kid was in a hurry to get somewhere, wasn't watching, and ran out in front of the car." They stopped talking while Myrtle brought his coffee and refilled Mark's cup. "Did you tell him about what Sammy said to me?" Stump nodded. "Sheriff says the kid was probably in shock and talking out of his head."

They were silent for a minute and then Mark asked, "Is

that what you believe?" Shaking his head, Stump replied, "I just don't know what to believe. The facts say it was a tragic accident, but my gut keeps telling me there's more to it." Mark replied, "For what it's worth, I agree with your gut." Stump leaned back and looked across the room as if he were looking out into the future. Mark did not speak so as not to distract him. He knew the man was just as frustrated as he was about Sammy's death. Maybe more so. Pushing his chair back, he said, "Preacher, I've heard it said that the good a person does outlives them. Sammy Garber was a good kid who did some good things. I guess we'll just have to be satisfied with that." Leaving fifty cents on the table, he left.

~

He had made an appointment to see Riley Barber and discuss attending seminary. As he walked into the church office, the secretary turned and called through an open door, "Rev. Thomas is here." The friendly voice in the office called out, "Come in, come in." He led Mark into his office and said he would be just a minute and stepped out to give some papers to the secretary. Mark walked over and looked at the diplomas hanging on the wall: a bachelor's degree from Carson-Newman College; and a master's and a doctor's degrees from New Orleans Baptist Theological Seminary. He envied those last two diplomas. Barber closed the door and, as if he could read Mark's mind, said, "It's not the degree you earn that's important. It's what you learn while earning the degree that's important."

Seeing Mark's somewhat puzzled look, he laughed and continued. "Mark, those diplomas have never added a thing to my ministry or sermons. It's what I learned in the classroom to get the diploma that has enhanced and strengthened my ministry and preaching." That made sense to Mark.

Pointing Mark to a chair, Barber sat down behind his desk. Leaning back, he propped his elbows on the chair arms, placed his hands together, almost in a prayer position, and asked, "Why do you want to go to seminary?" Mark told him he felt limited in his ministry, especially his preaching, due to his lack of theological training. He struggled with interpreting the scriptures and sermon preparation.

"I want to learn more about the Biblical languages and the proper interpretation and application of the doctrines."

Riley Barber smiled and said, "So you want to study hermeneutics, homiletics, and the other disciplines taught in seminary?" Seeing Mark's puzzled look, he laughed and said, "Those are just big words for what you study in seminary." He asked if Mark preferred which seminary to attend. "I would like to get some information on your seminary." With a big smile, Barber said, "Great, great. I think you would enjoy New Orleans." Mark asked if he could help him. "It just so happens, the man who oversees admissions is a long-time friend. I will call and tell him what you need. Where did you get your B.A.?" Mark told him Valdosta State College. "Excellent. Why don't you go ahead and get a transcript? I'm certain they will require one."

Mark then asked about the possibility of finding a part-time church to pastor if he did go to New Orleans. "Just so happens, my friend can handle that too. When are you thinking about going?" When Mark replied possibly in September, Barber suggested. "Don't wait until August to try and find a part-time church. Everyone is trying to find one and there are only so many churches. If you decide to go, go in July if possible. You stand a better chance of finding a church." He told Mark he would contact him when he had the information. As he turned to go, Mark asked if their conversation could be kept confidential. He didn't want to alarm the members of Gentry Baptist Church. Flashing his big smile, Barber replied, "I can't even remember why you came to see me!" They shared a laugh and Mark thanked him again for his help. "Mark, that's at the heart of ministry, helping others. Glad to do it." Helping others, the heart of ministry. He would have to remember that statement.

~

Because the church did not have a pastor's office, Mark didn't go to the church during the week unless something had to be done or someone needed to see him. After church one Sunday morning in January, Charlie Parker asked to see him during the week. "How about tomorrow at 2:00?" Charlie said that would be fine. After Charlie's retirement, he and his wife, Dolly, had started a personal ministry to the widows and elderly in the church—driving them to doctor appointments, taking them to buy groceries, running errands, doing minor repairs. Dolly had died three years ago, succumbing to the effects of diabetes that she'd ignored.

When Charlie entered the church, Mark could tell he was troubled. They sat facing one another on a back pew and Charlie spoke. "Preacher, I hope you won't be offended by what I'm about to share with you." Mark tensed, wondering what would offend him. "Preacher, Sarah Hughes and I are getting married, but we aren't going to ask you to do the wedding." This was news! There had been no indication that Charlie and Sarah had been seeing each other. As far as Mark could tell, Charlie's relationship with Sarah had been as a friend and fellow church member. Talk about a secret romance. They were in church every Sunday and gave no indication of a romantic relationship. Charlie continued. "At our age, we don't need a fancy wedding." Each month, the church recognized everyone having a birthday that month. If he remembered correctly, Charlie was seventy-five and Sarah about the same age. "What we want is just a small ceremony with our children present. Sarah has a nephew that's a preacher in Waycross and we've asked him to do the ceremony. I hope you understand." Mark could tell it was bothering Charlie to tell him this. "I understand, and I think what you are doing is best for the two of you." The older man breathed a sigh of relief. "Preacher, I want you to know we like you and wouldn't want to hurt your feelings for anything in the world."

Mark extended his hand. "Charlie, I'm not hurt or offended. I'm really happy for you and Sarah." Charlie paused as if debating whether to say something else. Mark silently waited, seeing the troubled look return to Charlie's face. "Preacher, I hope you won't believe the gossip that's going around that I am only marrying for sex." Mark could not have been more astonished if a semi-truck had just driven down the center aisle of the church. After the initial shock, he almost laughed but saw the agonized look on the older man's face. The idea of two people in their mid-seventies marrying just for sex. Controlling himself, he said, "Charlie, believe me when I say I would never think that."

"It's that Sadie Hightower. She heard we were getting married and started her gossiping. Preacher, it's embarrassing." Mark's heart went out to this man and his wife to be. As far as he knew, Charlie and Sarah were good moral people. What kind of person gossips and spreads lies that hurt the reputations of innocent people? Then he quickly remembered the gossip she started about Gail and him. "Charlie," he said, "you and Sarah have nothing to be ashamed of. Hold your head high and don't let her gossip bother you." Close to tears, the older man thanked Mark for his time and understanding. As he locked the door, Mark remembered the words of Jesus, *"For ye have the poor always with you."* With people like Sadie Hightower in the world, there should be a verse that said, *"For ye have the gossips always with you."*

It was the last Saturday of January and they were eating at Shoney's. They had placed their order and were holding hands across the table. Suddenly, without any forethought, Mark asked, "Gail, will you marry me?" She closed her eyes and tightened her lips. Mark's heart rate increased, and questions raced through his mind. Did he do this all wrong? Was it romantic enough? Should he have waited? Then she opened her eyes, which were watery, smiled, squeezed his hands tightly and said, "Yes."

His apprehension was quickly replaced with a joy he didn't think he could contain. He had an impulse to jump and shout to everyone in the restaurant, *"We are getting married!"* Since that behavior didn't seem appropriate for a minister of the gospel, he refrained. So they just sat, held hands, and smiled at one another. Then he realized that they were sitting in the same booth as that day he accidently bumped into her. When he brought this to her attention and called it a coincidence, she shook her head and said, "Mark, I don't believe God does anything coincidently." He had to agree with that. She said, "Mark, we have a lot to talk about." Grinning, he asked, "Do we have to do it all now?" They were laughing when the server brought their food.

Finishing their meal, she said, "Well, let's go home and tell my mother and call your mother." Pulling out of the parking lot, he said, "I've got two phone calls to make—Mom and Bill Swain.

Ran Like Joseph

Chapter 15

They agreed it best to tell the congregation to avoid any erroneous stories going around Gentry or, in the case of Sadie Hightower, erroneous gossip. When the worship service ended, Mark motioned everyone to sit. He then announced that he and Gail would be getting married. "We don't have a definite date set, but when we do, you'll be the first to know." Realizing what he had said, he grinned and corrected himself. "Okay, not the first to know, but shortly thereafter." The response to his announcement was smiles, nods, and some of the women reaching for a handkerchief or tissue to wipe a tear. *Do they always do that, he wondered?*

As he left the platform to walk to the vestibule, he stopped at Gail's pew and motioned for her to come. Taking her arm, he escorted her to the vestibule. With some alarm, she whispered, "What's wrong?" He whispered back, "Nothing's wrong. I just want you at my side from now on."

She smiled and gave him a quick hug, just as the deacon finished the benediction. Then Gail was besieged by women asking to see her ring. *Her ring!* He hadn't thought about a ring since his proposal wasn't planned. *What kind of an idiot asks a girl to marry him without an engagement ring?* If embarrassment were fatal, he would have been dead in seconds. The next few minutes were the most miserable of his life. He alternated between embarrassment and feeling like an imbecile. If a hole had opened in the floor and swallowed him up, he would have been grateful.

When everyone had left, he said, "Gail, I'm so sorry." She put her finger against his lips. "Sweetheart, it's okay. Don't be so upset. I know you'll get me a ring." Then with a teasing look, she added, "Maybe even a bigger one now." He groaned, and she laughed and hugged him. "I'm just kidding. Now let's go eat dinner."

He was silent on the ride to her house but vowed that he would go to Valdosta the next day and buy a ring.

True to his word, he went to Valdosta the next morning, arriving thirty minutes before the stores opened. Waiting in his car, he contemplated his impending purchase and realized he had no idea what an engagement ring would cost. And what size ring did Gail wear? And what size diamond should he buy? When the door was unlocked and he entered, his confusion was spiraling out of control.

The salesman led him to a glassed-in counter that held dozens of diamond rings. For the next half hour, Mark looked at the various sizes and settings. He was amazed there were so many to choose from. This didn't help his confusion. He finally settled on a ring and asked the price. When the salesman said, $495.00, he almost fell over backwards. *That was more than two months of his salary!* He decided to try another jewelry store around the block. Perhaps their prices were lower. He found a similar ring, but it was only $5.00 less. So there it was. Almost $500.00 for an engagement ring.

He returned to Gentry without the ring he had vowed to buy. It was not a happy ride. True, he had some money he was saving for seminary tuition. Should he use it to buy the ring? Should he finance the ring? What was that term the salesman used? Easy pay? Halfway home, he started praying aloud, just talking to God, asking that somehow, someway, he be able to afford a ring for Gail. He recited James 1:5, *"If any of you lack wisdom, let him ask of God, that giveth to all men liberally, and upbraideth not; and it shall be given him."* He didn't want to do anything based solely on emotion or that was financially unwise.

Stopping at the traffic light, he remembered he needed a few groceries, so he made a left turn to Tuttle's Grocery. Miriam Tuttle truly had the gift of discernment. She could instinctively read a person's mood, especially when it was so different from their normal demeanor. As Mark selected his groceries, she knew something was bothering him and in her own unobtrusive way, she asked. He told her about his failed attempt to buy an engagement ring. She responded in her usual optimistic manner. "Surely there's a way for you to buy that ring." He just shook his head glumly and reached for his wallet to pay for his groceries. As she handed him his change, she exclaimed, "I know! The Blue Book." He shook his head. "What's the Blue Book?" She was getting more excited by the moment. "It's a wholesale catalog from one of our suppliers. We don't use it much, but I think it has jewelry in it." Still not understanding, he asked her what that had to do with his situation. "Preacher," she said, "The prices are wholesale, not retail. We can order a ring for you at the wholesale cost." Now he was getting excited.

She led him back to the small room they used as an office. Reaching to a shelf she took down a large catalog and placed it on the desk. Flipping through the pages, she came to a jewelry section. "Look through here and see if there's anything you like." Sure enough, there were rings similar to the ones he saw in Valdosta. And just like those rings, the suggested retail price was $495.00. Pointing to the one he liked, he asked what the wholesale cost would be. She quickly calculated and replied, $265.00. He couldn't believe it. "Are you sure?" he asked. She assured him that was the wholesale price. "We could order it for you, and it would be here in a week. The only thing is, we have to pay cash when it's delivered." Quickly he calculated. He still had the $100.00 gift from the church, so he would only have to spend $165.00 of his savings. "Order it," he said. She said she would place the order that day and then added with a smile, "I won't tell anyone." Spontaneously, he hugged her. "Mrs. Miriam, you are an answer to prayer." A prayer that was answered in less than an hour. Mark left the store with a bounce in his step and a song in his heart. Gail would have her ring!

The following Monday, the ring arrived at Tuttle's, Mark paid for it, and then he and Miriam Tuttle opened the package. "Oh Preacher," she said, "It's beautiful." He couldn't wait until 3:30 when he would meet Gail at the restaurant to discuss church business.

He made a point to get to the restaurant before Gail did. Placing the ring box on the table at her seat, he covered it with a napkin. When she arrived, she seemed a bit flustered and didn't notice it at first. "Anything wrong?" he asked. "Just trying to get my classes ready for testing and most of them are not in the mood." When Myrtle brought two Cokes to the table, Gail noticed the napkin. "What's this?" she asked and lifted the napkin. When she saw the ring box, she paused and looked at Mark. "Go ahead," he said, "open it." When Gail saw the ring, she exclaimed, "Mark!" and startled

Myrtle who was cleaning a table. She hurried over just in time to see Gail slip the ring on her finger. Realizing what had happened, Myrtle started laughing and crying at the same time. She hugged Gail and then hugged Mark. Wiping tears with the edge of her apron, she said, "That's got to be the most romantic thing that's ever happened in this place."

The following Sunday, Gail proudly showed off her engagement ring and he didn't feel quite so idiotic.

~

Riley Barber had notified him that he had received the information Mark requested from New Orleans Baptist Theological Seminary. Riley was able to explain the forms, answer questions, and offer some valuable insights. Mark genuinely liked the man. It was easy to see why his congregation loved him. Besides his natural friendliness, he had the ability to encourage people. His church was several times larger than Mark's, but he treated him as an equal. As Mark rose to leave, Riley made an offer that surprised Mark. "Would you like to meet on a weekly basis and discuss the ministry?" Riley saw a young man that needed to be mentored, much like someone had mentored him thirty years before. Mark readily accepted, and they agreed on Tuesday afternoon.

Mark was somewhat hesitant to discuss the subject of attending seminary with Gail, but knew he had to at some point. It was something that would affect their future and it was only right that she should help make any decision.

When he arrived at her house on Saturday, he asked if they could do something different than attend a movie and eat at Shoney's. "Gail, there are things we need to talk about." With a raised eyebrow, she retorted, "That's my line." Then she saw how serious he was. Moving to the porch, he turned a rocking chair, so he could face her as he talked. He asked her to hear him out before she asked any questions or started a discussion. As briefly and as clearly as he could, he told her about his desire to attend seminary, wanting to do all he could to prepare himself for the calling God had placed on his life. He wanted her to know that it was not a spur of the moment idea, but something that had been in his mind since before graduation from college. As he continued to pray about it over the past few months, the desire had not diminished but had increased. He

concluded by telling her about his visit with Riley Barber and the information he had received from New Orleans Baptist Theological Seminary.

When he finished, she stared out across the yard and was quiet for an extended time, at least it seemed extended to him. "Mark, I'm not only joining my life with yours, I'm also joining my life with God's call on your life. We cannot separate the two. Yes, there is a part of me that wants to stay here where everything is familiar, but I know that's not possible."

"Sweetheart," he said, "we would only be in New Orleans for three years." "And what then Mark? Where would we go?" Very quietly, he answered, "Wherever God leads." She started to rock and said, "You know, we talk about following God, but there's a big difference in saying it and doing it. We sing the hymn, *Wherever He Leads, I'll Go*, but do we mean it?" Nodding his head, he replied, "My preacher back home used to say that Baptists lied most when they sang."

She asked when he, or they, would leave to attend seminary. "Gail, if possible, in the summer. I would like to start classes in September." She leaned forward, took his hands, and said, "Then we have a lot to pray about." She was right. They did have a lot to pray about.

~

The Tuesday afternoon sessions became one of the highlights of Mark's week. After lunch he drove to Tadlock and the two men would spend a couple of hours discussing various aspects of the ministry. They followed a simple pattern: Mark would make a list of questions he wanted to ask, and Riley made a list of subjects he felt would be beneficial to discuss. One day, Riley surprised Mark when he said the topic was criticism and conflict. He asked Mark if he had dealt with these things. Mark recounted the problem with Stella Boyd. Riley responded, "That's good and bad. Bad that you had to deal with it so early in your tenure at Gentry, but good that it turned out the way it did." He reflected and continued. "You know you put yourself in jeopardy when you offered to resign? Suppose that had happened?"

Mark said, "I was aware of that possibility. That could have been the end of my ministry in Gentry. But I've made a personal commitment to the Lord, that I will never allow myself to be the point of controversy or division in a church." The older pastor looked at Mark with a newfound regard. "Mark, I made that same commitment early in my ministry and I believe the Lord has honored it. Not that there haven't been some rough spots along the way."

"Riley," he asked, "how have you been able to have such lengthy tenures as a pastor? It seems like some pastors are moving every couple of years. What's your secret?" Flashing his big smile, he replied, "There's no secret, as you call it. I was given some advice years ago and I'm convinced it works: Always keep a committee between you and the church." Mark said, "I don't understand."

"Mark, allow the people to function in the roles to which

they were elected. Let them make decisions and bring recommendations to the church. Lead them but allow them to do their work. It will take a lot of pressure off you and reduce the criticism. Let me give you an example. Two years ago, we discussed remodeling and updating our sanctuary. It was showing some age. The Building and Grounds Committee had a contractor create a diagram of the proposed changes, along with a cost estimate. They made the recommendation to the church and the majority voted in favor of it. There was a small group that opposed it and individuals came to me with their criticism. I reminded them that it wasn't my recommendation and that the majority had already voted to proceed. That meant I couldn't do anything to stop it but if they felt that strongly, they could come to the next business meeting and make a motion to not remodel. Not a one was willing to do that, and we proceeded with the remodeling."

Mark leaned back and mused, "Wouldn't it be nice if there were no critics in the church." Riley erupted in laughter. "Like my granddaddy used to say, 'fleas come with the dog'."

The thing Mark admired the most in Barber's office was the bookshelves that lined the walls, filled with books. Mark's library consisted of a three-shelf bookcase and it wasn't full. He asked how many and the answer was, perhaps a thousand. When Mark expressed doubt that he would ever own that many, Riley encouraged him to buy books and continue to read throughout the duration of his ministry. "I have no doubt that has tremendously benefited my ministry. Some preachers stop studying when they complete seminary, evidently thinking they know all they need to know." He suggested Mark visit secondhand bookstores where he could buy books at a fraction of their retail cost. Mark was completely caught off guard when Riley told him he could borrow any books he needed.

As they continued their Tuesday sessions, a close bond developed between the older and younger man. In Mark, Riley saw the young pastor he once was. In Riley, Mark saw the pastor he wanted to be.

Ran Like Joseph

Chapter 16

It was the second week of March and Mark was working on a sermon when someone knocked at his door. He opened it to see Fred Hewett, pastor of the Methodist Church. Fred had retired early from a large church in Orlando due to a heart condition. He lived in Gentry where he preached on the first and third Sundays of the month and preached in the adjacent county on the second and fourth Sundays. When there was a fifth Sunday, he would worship at one of the other churches in Gentry. "Come in Fred. Good to see you." He motioned his guest to one of the easy chairs. Mark didn't often have visitors in his apartment and was curious as to why Fred had come. "Mark, it's my job to plan the community Easter sunrise service" Mark nodded, being aware of the service held at the school baseball field. "You probably aren't aware of a sort of tradition we have in Gentry. The newest preacher in town is asked to preach at the sunrise service." This was news to Mark, and he started to protest. "But Fred, I've only been here a few months, and you other preachers are more experienced than I am; and, well, I've never preached a sunrise service."

The pleasant faced pastor smiled and replied, "Mark, there's a first time for everything and I've heard you preach enough to know that you will do a good job." Mark started to offer another objection, but Fred raised a hand and said, "You aren't going to do that Moses thing are you? When he tried to avoid going back to Egypt to lead the exodus." They both laughed and Mark said he would be honored to preach the sunrise service. "Fine, fine," Fred said. "You know what this means don't you?" Mark said. When Fred shook his head no, Mark replied, "It means I've got to prepare two Easter sermons." Fred thanked him and assured him he would do fine. "We'll be in touch," he said as he left.

A sunrise service meant two Easter sermons. Maybe Riley Barber could help him out. He had just resumed studying when there was another knock. He was thinking how unusual it was. Two visitors in one morning. He didn't have two a month. Opening the door, he saw Harley Bass. "Preacher, it's Mrs. Fry. She's in a bad way. Jeanette is taking her to the hospital in Tadlock. Thought you would want to know."

"What's happened?" he asked. Harley told him

Jeanette had taken some food over, and Mrs. Fry wasn't responsive. According to Howard she had been that way since the day before. "I'll see you at the hospital," he said.

It was a long afternoon. His memory of the waiting room was not a pleasant one. When he did visit the Tadlock hospital, he made a point to avoid the waiting room so as not to be reminded of Sammy Garber's death. Howard was there, along with Harley and Jeanette. This time, no one had to prompt him to pray. It was the first thing he did after they related what the doctor had said. Mrs. Fry was severely dehydrated, a result of not getting enough fluids, and possibly some other issues. Tests were being done. So they waited.

He thought about something Riley Barber had told him in one of their recent sessions as they discussed pastoral ministry. "Mark, he said, "never underestimate the importance of your presence when a family has a problem. There are times you will feel inadequate, not having the answers, not being able to do anything to help. But as a pastor, your presence at those times is immeasurable. You are God's representative to them. Your prayers and your words of comfort mean more than you know. You are their pastor and they need you." Mark was beginning to realize that Riley was teaching him practical things that he would never learn in a classroom.

Shortly after five o'clock, he went to the pay phone in the hall to call Mrs. Smith and tell her he may be late for supper, and for Gail and her to go ahead and eat. "Son, we'll keep some warm for you." In public, she still called him Preacher or Rev. Thomas. In private it was Mark or Son. He couldn't have chosen a better woman to be his future mother-in-law. But then, he didn't make the choice. God did!

When he returned to the waiting room, the doctor was talking with Howard. Tilly was going to be okay but would need to be hospitalized for a couple of days. Harley and Jeanette would take Howard home and see that he ate. "I'll bring him back tomorrow to visit," Jeanette said. Mark nodded, so grateful for people like Harley and Jeanette who responded to the needs of others without being asked. He could only wonder what a church could accomplish if all members lived out their faith as these two did.

He went to bed that night, fully expecting to have the nightmare about Sammy Garber's death due to his time in the waiting room at the Tadlock hospital. To his surprise, it didn't occur. It would be a week before he had another one. The nightmare never changed. He was holding Sammy who begged him to save him; his grip slipped, and Sammy fell screaming into the dark hole. The screams always woke him.

~

The following Tuesday, Mark told Riley about the sunrise service and asked if he had any suggestions for a sermon. Reaching to a shelf, he took a notebook labeled, Easter Sermons. "Mark, this is something I wish I had started earlier in my ministry. Keep a notebook with your sermon notes and outlines." He then proceeded to flip the pages, commenting on different Easter sermons he had preached over the years. Stopping at a page, he said, "Okay, here it is. I preached this one a few years ago." He removed the page and handed it to Mark. "Don't preach it verbatim. Use it for a guide. Read the scripture passage, read your commentaries, and develop your own sermon. Give it back when you finish." Scanning the page of neatly typed notes, he knew he had just learned another lesson from the "School of Riley".

As he and Gail began to discuss plans, she said they needed a "countdown calendar" and asked if he knew what she was referring to. Pretending ignorance, he allowed her to continue explaining. Taking a calendar, she said, "You establish a target date for your goal and then work backwards, filling in the necessary steps to complete the goal." Nodding he understood, he asked, "And on what date does Miss Smith become Mrs. Thomas?" She pretended evasiveness which led to some facetiousness. "Okay, seriously, Gail, I can't take you to New Orleans unless we're married and I'm not going without you." With a sly smile, she replied, "Then I guess we'll have to get married." He couldn't resist kissing her. "Gail," he continued, "getting married is not a step in the plan. It's the most important thing in my future. Our future." Now it was her turn to pretend ignorance. "You understand, Reverend Thomas, I've never planned a wedding before." He grinned and replied, "Neither have I, but there's a first time for everything. Now, let's set a date."

For the next thirty minutes, they pored over the calendar, discussing what needed to be done in order to wed and move to New Orleans. Gail wanted to wait until school was ended to have the wedding, so they could have time for a honeymoon. School ended the last Friday of May. They could be married the first Saturday in June, honeymoon, return home, and then depart for New Orleans. Looking at the calendar, Mark said he needed to decide what date to inform the church and resign. "Oh Mark, that's going to be so hard for them. The people love you and they will be terribly disappointed." Maybe he needed to talk to Riley Barber and get his advice on how to resign from a church. Was there an easy way? Probably not. "We can decide on that later," he said.

As Gail circled the date, June 5, she showed some panic. "Mark, we have less than three months to plan a wedding!" Being totally ignorant of weddings, he shrugged. "Is that a problem?" She gave him a look that conveyed, *I can't believe you!* "My dear husband to be, a wedding doesn't just happen. I have to buy a dress, choose my attendants, plan for decorating the church, get someone to bake a wedding cake..." She stopped in mid-sentence. "But, I suppose we should tell our mothers first."

Mrs. Smith was vacuuming her bedroom and to get her attention, Gail unplugged the vacuum. "Mom, we've set a date!" Dropping the vacuum hose, she clapped her hands together, her usual response to anything that excited her. "Oh, honey, when?" When told June 5, she got that same look of panic. "Gail, that means we have less than three months to plan a wedding!" Mark couldn't help but think, *here we go again.*

"Mother, there's something else we need to discuss." The three of them returned to the dining table where they proceeded to share their plans of moving to New Orleans. The joyous expression on Mrs. Smith's face quickly changed. Her emotions were in turmoil--the joy of her daughter's wedding and her disappointment that she would be moving hundreds of miles away. "Mom, I know this is a lot to give you at one time." Placing a hand on her mother's hand she said, "I'm sorry."

There was a silence before her mother spoke. "No need to be sorry child. I figured that you would marry one day and possibly move away. I guess my sadness is because you are my only daughter and I've so enjoyed these last two years you've been back home." With a change of expression, she looked at them and said, "The important thing is that you obey the Lord. Son, if you believe this is what God wants you to do, then you need to do it." Gail then asked her mother to keep the seminary part confidential. "Well," she said with a smile, "Daughter, we have a wedding to plan." Gail turned to Mark and said, "Why don't you go call your mother?"

On Sunday, at the conclusion of the service, Mark asked Gail to join him on the platform and they officially informed the congregation of their wedding date. The response was smiles, nods, and women reaching for their handkerchiefs and tissues.

Gail and her mother began in earnest to plan the wedding. Some decisions were easy to make. Her brother, Robert, would give her away and his wife, June, would be her matron of honor. She decided not to have any other attendants, desiring to keep it simple. That meant Mark needed a best man and that could only be Bill Swain. The name wasn't familiar to Mrs. Smith, so he explained their college friendship and that it was Bill who had prodded him into asking Gail for a date. "Since he was instrumental in getting us to this point, I want him to be a part of the wedding."

Who would perform the wedding ceremony? Gail didn't

have a preference since her favorite preacher from childhood was deceased. As they considered possibilities, he suggested Riley Barber and Gail readily agreed. Gail informed him that she and her mother would be going to Valdosta on Saturday to shop for a wedding dress. He could go along for the ride or stay at home. He wisely chose to stay home and go fishing with Paul Slocum.

The next time he met with Riley Barber, he asked if he would consider performing their wedding. "Mark, I would be honored to do it." That led to a discussion about performing weddings and Riley gave him some resources.

"There are two occasions when people need spiritual guidance and advice, Mark. Weddings and funerals. You will discover that those two occasions will help create strong bonds between you and the people. Take some time to prepare outlines for funeral sermons because you have short notice."

Mark and Gail had stopped the Monday meeting at the restaurant to handle church correspondence and other items. They did it on Monday night when he went for supper. As he walked up the steps the first Monday of April, Gail met him with a kiss and, "I've got a surprise for you."

"Big surprise or little surprise?" he asked. "You'll be the judge of that. Your mother is coming for Easter!" This was a surprise. He hadn't talked to his mother about coming for Easter and she hadn't mentioned it in her letters. "And how did this come to be?" he asked. She answered, "Mom thought it would be nice to have her here for Easter, so she called her last night and she's coming. Mom is so excited about having her here."

As they entered the house, Mrs. Smith called out from the kitchen, "Hi Son, wash up. Supper's ready." She treated him as if he was her son. After he asked the blessing, she said, "I'm so glad Ruth agreed to come. It will be so nice to have us all together to celebrate Easter."

At times Gail had papers to grade, so he and Mrs. Smith engaged in conversation as they watched television. Their conversations revealed to him what a truly Godly woman she was, and he could see that influence in Gail's life. She had moved past her temporary disappointment about their moving to New Orleans and was enthusiastic about Mark attending seminary and extending his education. One evening she told him, "Mark, you have the ability to simplify the scriptures so that people can better understand what you are preaching. Not every preacher can do that. Why, Son, I've heard some preachers use such big words that the apostle Paul would be confused. I hope you don't discard that style of preaching as you broaden your education. The greatest need of those of us who sit in the pew is to be taught what God revealed of himself in the Bible." Their conversations always gave him something to ponder.

Chapter 17

Easter dawned clear and somewhat cool. Not cold, but cool enough to require a jacket or coat. The sunrise service wasn't at sunrise, but at 7:00. Those attending sat in the baseball stands, and a lectern was placed at home plate for the song leader and preacher. The churches provided coffee and donuts.

He met Gail and their mothers for a quick cup of coffee before the service started. The crowd of combined churches numbered almost three hundred. Their singing was enthusiastic, and everyone was in great spirits. Mark was glad his voice projected well so that the people could hear him.

He used the outline Riley Barber had shared with him. The scripture was Mark 16:1-4, focusing on the question asked by the women on their way to the tomb: *"Who shall roll us away the stone from the door of the sepulcher?"* He posed three aspects of the stone that covered the tomb of Jesus.

(1) It Was a Symbol of Sorrow. Death brings sorrow.

(2)It Was a Symbol of Sin. Jesus died for our sin, paying a debt he did not owe because we owed a debt we could not pay.

(3) It Was a Symbol of Separation. Sin separated man from God, but the resurrection of Jesus Christ removes the barrier of separation.

As he continually scanned over the crowd, he could see his mother's pride as she listened. Afterwards, he received many compliments on the sermon, with several saying it may have been the best Easter sunrise message they had ever heard. He was grateful for Riley Barber's thoughtfulness and generosity.

The Easter service at church was equally special. The children's choir and the choir sang, and Gail sang one of his favorites, *Were You There?* Hearing her beautiful voice was another reminder of how blessed he was that she would be his wife. He glanced at the two mothers', faces radiant as Gail sang. Anyone observing them would have thought they were lifelong friends.

Mark's message in the church service was Matthew's account of the women going to the tomb, but his emphasis was on the statement the angel made: *"And go quickly, and tell."* He challenged the congregation that they had something to go tell the world:

> (1)Go Tell That the Tomb is Empty

> (2)Go Tell That Jesus is Alive

> (3)Go Tell There is a Way of Salvation

On the first verse of the invitation hymn, Elmer and Janie Lane stepped out of their pew and came down the aisle. Grabbing Mark's hand, he simply said, "Preacher, I'm trusting in Jesus." Janie recommitted her life to Christ. When the invitation hymn ended, Mark said, "My friend Elmer has given his life to Christ," and there was a spontaneous eruption of "Amen" across the church. Mark then asked the children to come and stand with their parents and the sight was one that the members of Gentry Baptist Church would cherish for a long time. There wasn't a dry eye in the church.

Mom Smith's Easter dinner was a masterpiece-baked ham, candied yams, peas, macaroni and cheese, biscuits, and coconut cake for dessert. After the meal, he told his mother about the plans to attend seminary. It was not as traumatic for her since he had left home at eighteen, almost eight years ago. She was pleased that he was continuing his education. "Son, God has a purpose for your life. I've always believed that. Your daddy did too. He would be so proud of you and I am too." He walked over, hugged her, and thanked her for always believing in him.

There were no evening services on Easter, so Mark settled back on the couch, intending to relax when Gail asked, "Mom Ruth, did you bring the photos?" So the afternoon was spent looking at photos of Mark when he was a kid. Gail laughed and kidded him and at one point jokingly said, "Oh, I'm certain I waved at this boy one of those times we passed through Bishop." Looking at the photo she was holding, he guessed he must have been about ten, skinny, with a buzz haircut, barefoot, and missing a couple of teeth. "Yes," he joked back, "I can see how he would make a lasting impression."

His mother planned to stay for a week at Mom Smith's invitation and was included in the ongoing wedding preparations. Mark was especially busy the week after Easter with his morning study time, hospital visits to Tadlock and Valdosta, and his Tuesday afternoon session with Riley Barber. It was a relief that his mother had something to keep her busy and he didn't feel obligated to spend time with her. Each evening at supper she shared what they had accomplished during the day and her enthusiasm for the wedding was obvious. As he was her only child, this would be her only opportunity to help with a wedding as a parent. She had arrived on Thursday before Easter and planned to return home on the next Thursday and Mark was surprised when she announced that she would be staying a few more days at Rebecca's request, to help with the wedding plans. He was pleased the two women had become so close, knowing of situations where the in-laws didn't get along.

~

The Sunday after Easter, Nell Garber asked if he could come by for a visit and they agreed on Saturday morning. He had noticed that her demeanor had seemed to improve in recent weeks. She smiled a little more and participated in more conversations at church. Gail had noticed a difference in her behavior in the school cafeteria. Maybe she was conquering her grief and sorrow.

The following Saturday morning, he walked the several blocks to the small frame house and knocked on the door. She welcomed him in and thanked him for taking the time to visit. She poured coffee and congratulated him on the upcoming wedding. She told him, "I've known the Smiths for most of my life. Watched Gail grow up and come back here to teach. Preacher, I'm not just saying this to favor you. Gail is one of the finest, sweetest women God placed on this earth, at least around here. Sammy loved her as a teacher, and she gave him some extra help since he wanted to be a sportswriter. You are a blessed man to have her as your wife." She paused to take a sip of coffee and he could see she was gathering her thoughts.

"Preacher, these last few months have been terrible. There's no other way to describe it. Sammy was my life after his daddy died and when he died..." Her sentence trailed off into a silence and she reached for a tissue to wipe her tears. "I'm sorry Preacher." He patted her hand and assured her it was okay to express her grief. Regaining her composure, she continued. "A few weeks ago, you preached from the 23rd Psalm, about going through the valley of the shadow of death." He nodded, remembering the sermon. "Well, what you said started me to thinking. I took what you said and applied it to Sammy. He went through that dark valley, but he didn't go alone, Jesus went with him. And, like you said, he didn't stay in that valley, he just passed through it. And he came out on the other side, which is heaven. And now, he will be in the house of the Lord forever."

As she talked, a smile slowly came to her face. "Preacher, God has helped me accept what happened to

Sammy. I still don't understand why it had to happen, but I can see that I can trust God to take care of my Sammy. Am I making sense?" He told her she was making perfect sense. She went on to tell him how she hadn't touched Sammy's room since the day he died. Everything was just as it was the last time he left it. "Sammy was a neat boy," she said. "He made up his bed and straightened up his room every morning. Well, I've decided to clean out his room and get rid of what I don't need to keep, like these." She pointed to a stack of composition books on the table. "He loved to practice writing reports, he called them stories, of games he watched on television, especially baseball and football. 'Practicing' he said. These are things I'll probably throw away."

She stood and said, "It's lunch time. Will you stay and have a sandwich with me?" Mark was on the verge of declining her offer, wanting to get to Gail's house, but something in her eyes, almost pleading, made him change his mind. "Yes ma'am, I'd be delighted to stay."

"It won't take me but a few minutes," she said, and went to the kitchen. Mark moved the stack of composition books closer, picked up the top one and started to read. Sammy did have an ability to describe a sporting event in clear, concise terms. He was obviously a devoted sports fan and had an above average understanding of the different sports he wrote about. Who knows, Mark thought, he may have been the next Furman Bisher. Any sports fan who grew up in Georgia was acquainted with Bisher, the legendary sportswriter for the Atlanta Journal-Constitution.

When he picked up the fourth composition book, he read the first line and realized it was not a sports story but rather a personal journal, with entries about his summer activities, aspirations for his senior year in high school, and his relationship with Sue Kelly. Out of respect for Sammy's memory and privacy, he was about to close the composition book when an entry caught his eye.

"She is getting bolder in her advances and I must be careful when I am alone with her. She is a married woman and what she is suggesting is disgusting to me."

And then another entry.

"I don't know how much longer I can find ways to resist her. She is persistent. I must be careful and not go to the house if she is there alone. If all else fails, I will just have to run like Joseph."

Mark felt his heart racing. This was it! This was the explanation of why Sammy Garber was running! Wanda Kelly was trying to seduce him.

"Almost ready," Nell said from the kitchen. He quickly

slid the journal book under the others and pushed them back to the edge of the table. It was a struggle to contain his emotions and act normal. Nell came from the kitchen, carrying plates of tuna sandwiches and chips. She returned to get glasses of tea and cups of fruit. Mark wasn't sure of what he said as a blessing. His mind was in a turmoil. After lunch, he waited enough time so as not to be rude and then excused himself, telling her he had some errands to run. In a nonchalant way, he asked if he could borrow Sammy's journals and read some more of his sports stories. "You are welcome to them. I was just going to look at them and throw them away."

She walked him to the door, thanking him again and telling him how helpful his visit was. If she only knew how helpful, he thought. Within minutes he was back in his apartment, reading the journal again. There could be no doubt. Wanda Kelly was trying to seduce Sammy just like Potiphar's wife tried to seduce Joseph. Like Joseph, Sammy was resistant to her advances, knowing it was wrong. Like Joseph, he had to resort to running away from the seduction. The only difference was Joseph's running led him to prison. Sammy's running led to his death. That was the meaning of his final words--ran like Joseph. Like was the word that was incoherent. Ran *like* Joseph was what he was trying to say.

For the next hour, Mark re-thought the whole accident

scene, trying to imagine every little detail of that tragic night. Doyle and Sue were not home that fateful night, but Sammy didn't know that when he went to visit. Wanda must have been overly aggressive in her effort to seduce the young man and his only option was to run. He ran like Joseph. Tears began to stream down Mark's face as he thought about the resolve this young man had to resist the tempting advances of a married woman. *Sammy*, he thought, *you were a special young man. I wish I could have known you better.*

Now he knew why Wanda Kelly acted so strangely at the funeral, and why she left the room when he and Stump visited to discuss Sammy's death. She was responsible. It all made sense. Stump's puzzle, as he called it, was solved!

There was a knock at the door. It was Edith Cole. "Preacher, Gail just called to see if you were here and if anything was wrong." He had completely forgotten about Gail, their Saturday date, everything but Sammy's death. "No, everything's okay. I was reading and lost track of time. Thanks, Mrs. Cole."

He apologized to Gail for being late and she knew something was bothering him. "It's just Sammy's death. Sometimes it just gets the best of me." They drove to Valdosta and he tried to put on a good front but was only partly successful. Too late for the matinee, they walked around downtown and made a pretense of shopping. She bought some cosmetics and he a pair of socks. After their usual meal at Shoney's, he drove home but found it difficult to stay focused on the conversation. His mind continued to drift to that Blue Horse Composition book. Bidding her goodnight, he apologized for his mood. Hugging him, she said, "Mark, there will be ups and downs in our lives. I am here for you and I know you will be there for me. Together, we will get through whatever life brings." He squeezed her tightly, told her he loved her, and kissed her goodnight.

Lying in his bed, he pondered what to do with his discovery. And he prayed. Sunday was an ordeal. Trying his best, he went through the usual routine, hoping he would not betray his feelings. He smiled, he greeted, he conversed, and he preached. The worst part was when Nell Garber asked him what he thought of Sammy's sports stories.

When he got home Sunday night, he read and re-read Sammy's entries about Wanda Kelly's advances. He became aware of an anger building in him that was unlike anything he had ever known. It was almost to the point of a hatred for Wanda Kelly. There had been times that he had been angry at different people but never to the point of hating them.

He stopped reading and fell to his knees, asking God to forgive him and give him some direction for handling the situation. Physically and emotionally exhausted, he went to bed. It was after midnight when he fell asleep.

Jimmy Deas

Chapter 18

On Monday morning, he knew what he would do: confront Wanda Kelly. Waiting until 10:00 so that Doyle would be at work and Sue at school, he walked to the Kelly house and knocked on the door. Opening the door, she said, "Why Reverend Thomas, this is a surprise. Won't you come in?" As she led him to a chair, she asked if she could get him something to drink and he declined. She flashed him a big smile and asked, "What can I do for you?" Wanda Kelly had the looks and figure that appealed to men. She had sexual charm and she knew it and knew how to use it. She was what his mother would call "a natural born flirt."

"Mrs. Kelly," he started to say. She interrupted, "Call me Wanda." He continued. "Mrs. Kelly, I've come to talk to you about Sammy's death." The expression on her face hardened but she said nothing. Mark then opened the composition book and read Sammy's entries. Looking at her he said, "Mrs. Kelly, you were trying to seduce Sammy and he resisted you. He came over here that night to see Sue, not knowing she had gone to Valdosta. You tried to seduce him, and he ran to get away from you and was killed. Mrs. Kelly, you are responsible for Sammy Garber's death and this proves it."

She was scared and it showed. There was a long silence as they stared at one another. Then she asked him to read Sammy's entries again. After he did, a defiant smile formed on her face. "Preacher, you don't have any proof as you call it. My name is not mentioned. This house is not mentioned. And I say that Sammy wasn't here that night." Mark was incredulous at her response. The gall of the woman. She continued. "Sounds to me like he had a sexual fantasy. Or it could have been another woman who was trying to seduce him." Raising her voice, she said, "You have no proof. Now leave and don't you ever come back here again."

Mark stood and walked to the door. "Mrs. Kelly, I'm leaving but I assure you, I will not let this rest. You are responsible for Sammy's death as surely as if you pushed him in front of that car." She screamed, "Get out!"

When Stump Harris came home for lunch, Mark was

waiting on his front porch. "Well, look what the cat drug up. Come on in and we'll have some lunch." Mark shook his head. "Lunch can wait. This is important." Stump plopped down in a rocker and said, "Fire away." Mark proceeded to show him the composition book and told of his visit to Wanda Kelly. "Stump, this is it! Now we know why he was running. Your puzzle is solved. Now what can we do about it?"

Stump lit another cigarette and rocked. Finally, he said, "Preacher, she's right. We have no proof. It's all circumstantial. He doesn't mention her name or the house. A good defense lawyer would tear that to pieces. Fact is, there's not enough there to arrest her."

"But Stump, it all makes sense. Doyle and Sue weren't at home and he was running from the direction of the Kelly house. And his last words. He was trying to tell me why he was running. Like Joseph in the Bible, he was running from the advances of a married woman."

The other man nodded in agreement. "What makes sense to you and me still wouldn't make sense in a court of law. Like I said, a good defense lawyer would tear that to pieces. Like she said, he could have been writing about some sexual fantasy or it could have been another woman. Preacher, as much as I hate to say it, there's nothing we can do."

Mark sputtered, "But...but we know it is the truth." Harris agreed. Leaning back in his rocker, with resignation in his voice, Mark said, "So, it means she goes free." The other man nodded, "Afraid so." Mark felt anger building. "So, we solve the mystery but there is no justice for Sammy." Shaking his head, Stump surprised Mark by saying, "I didn't say that. Doesn't the Bible say that vengeance belongs to the Lord and he will pay?" Mark nodded. "Preacher, I'm not as schooled on the Bible as you are, but I do believe that ultimately everyone pays for their crimes and wrongdoings. Wanda Kelly may not have to answer for what she did in a court of law but one day, she will answer to a higher authority." This was a side of Stump Harris Mark had not seen. He was somewhat amazed at the man's philosophy, or perhaps, theology of justice. And, deep down inside, he had to agree with the man. Justice may be delayed or even averted in this life, but the day of reckoning will come.

Both men rocked and contemplated what they had discussed. Then Stump said, "Preacher, you took a chance, going over there by yourself. That's a mean, evil woman. She could make some accusations, cause you some real problems." Mark responded, "I guess you're right, but didn't you ever take a chance to help someone who deserved it?" With a grunt, he responded, "Yep, I guess I have."

The two rocked in silence and Stump smoked through

a cigarette. As he was lighting a fresh one, he said, "Preacher, this is something we need to keep to ourselves. We don't need to tell anybody else."

"But, why? I'm not disputing, I just want to know why." Slowly rocking, Stump replied. "This is a small town. If people learned about this, they would turn against Wanda Kelly and that would cause problems for Doyle and Sue and they don't need that. And it would cause Nell Garber more grief and she doesn't need that." Taking a puff, he added, "And bottom line, it won't bring Sammy back. Telling this wouldn't solve anything but it would open up a whole new can of worms." Mark could see the wisdom in what the man was saying.

Standing, he flipped the cigarette butt into the yard. "Come on in and I'll fix you a baloney sandwich." Mark shook his head and replied, "No thanks. I'm just not hungry."

There was no energy in his step as he walked back home. The last three days had drained his emotions. It was so frustrating to have found the answer to Sammy Garber's death and to be powerless to do anything about it. At least he was the one who discovered Sammy's entries and not his mother. Some people would say it was a coincidence, but he knew better. God was gracious to Nell Garber.

On Saturday morning he went to the restaurant as

usual. As Myrtle was pouring his coffee, she asked, "Well, have you heard the latest news? Wanda Kelly has left Doyle. Went back to Valdosta, and word is, she's with another man." Mark almost spilled the hot coffee. "I'm sorry to hear that," he said, knowing he wasn't entirely truthful. "I hear Doyle's pretty broke up about it," she said. "But it was bound to happen sooner or later. He never should have married her in the first place. She was a man chaser if ever I saw one. I don't mean to judge, but there's nothing I would put past that woman." *Myrtle*, he thought, *you are right about that.*

Stump came in for coffee and Myrtle told him about Wanda Kelly. The two men listened and looked at one another without comment. When Myrtle moved away, Stump surprised Mark by saying, "Preacher, she can run away from Gentry, but she can't run away from her conscience. That woman is traveling fast down the hard road of life and she's going to crash one day."

~

Mark had chosen the third Sunday of May to announce his resignation. The previous Tuesday, it was the subject of his weekly session with Riley Barber. It would be another "first" of his first pastorate. As usual, Riley was informative and encouraging. "Mark, it's never easy to say goodbye to people you have come to know and love as a pastor. You have become a part of their lives and they of yours." The older pastor suggested that he explain to the congregation why he was leaving. "Knowing will help them accept it better. Folks hate to be left in the dark. And ask them to pray for you and Gail as you continue this journey of ministry. Make them feel they are a part of what God is doing in your life."

Mark had been dreading resigning, although he knew it was God's will for him to go to seminary. Leaving Riley's office, he felt better equipped to announce his resignation.

On Thursday morning, he was studying when someone knocked at his door. The door was open and through the screen, he recognized one of the boys from the senior class. Stepping to the door, Mark spoke and was told, "Mr. Barnes wants to see you." Barnes was the principal at Gentry High. Somewhat puzzled as to why the principal wanted to see him, he said, "Okay. Tell him about fifteen minutes." He reached a stopping point and closed his books.

As he walked into the principal's office, the secretary greeted him and told him to go on in. George Barnes stood to shake his hand and motioned to a chair. "Thanks for coming Reverend Thomas. The senior class is planning their graduation and baccalaureate programs and would like for you to preach the baccalaureate service." Mark was stunned. "I'm...I'm flattered. I'm honored to be asked, but why me? I don't have any connections to the class." None of the graduates was a member of his church. The principal reclined in his chair and replied, "Reverend Thomas, you became connected to that class the day you preached Sammy Garber's funeral. They are unanimous. They want you to preach their baccalaureate service." He considered for a minute and then agreed. Standing up and offering his hand, the principal said, "Fine, fine. I'll go down and tell them now. Someone from the senior class will contact you when they finish the plans."

That night he told Gail and her mother about the invitation to preach the senior class baccalaureate sermon. Mrs. Smith clapped her hands and Gail beamed and said, "I knew they wanted you to do it and I'm glad you accepted. You made a big impression on that group of students." Shaking his head, Mark said, "I'm surprised they would remember what I said at Sammy's funeral." Gail placed her elbows on the table and propped her head on her folded hands. "Sweetheart, it's not so much what you said, as what you did. The students know what you did for Sammy the night he died. That made a bigger impression on them than anything you said." Mrs. Smith nodded in agreement. "Son, people may forget what you said, but they will remember what you did."

Gail continued. "There's a similarity between teachers

and preachers. We often wonder if people are listening to us. It surprises me what my students do remember and how it influences them. With some people, it may be years before we are aware of the influence we had." Mark laughed and said, "You are so right. Most Sundays I wonder if you are really listening to me." Mrs. Smith laughed, and Gail playfully punched his shoulder. "Mark Thomas, you just wait," she said.

Sunday dawned as what was called a Florida postcard day, a bright sun and almost no clouds and pleasant weather. It was going to be a beautiful day weather-wise. Too bad I'm going to ruin it, Mark ruefully thought as he tied his tie. Everyone was in a good mood for worship and it showed. The singing was enthusiastic, Mark's sermon was well received, and to top it off, one of the youths made a profession of faith. He dreaded ruining the high spirits by resigning and briefly considered changing his mind about going to seminary. However, he looked at Gail and she seemed to understand his turmoil. She nodded affirmatively and his resolve returned.

After the invitation ended, he asked that the congregation be seated for a minute. Stepping back to the pulpit, he grabbed it with both hands for fear his hands would shake. His stomach might as well have been a washing machine the way it was churning. Taking a deep breath, he began to tell the congregation about his God-given desire to attend seminary. As he talked he could see the initial curiosity on faces turn to concern. Some of them intuitively knew where this was headed. He concluded by saying, "Therefore, in accordance with the by-laws of the church, I submit my resignation as your pastor, effective June 13th." The response was a chorus of "oh no's" and head shaking. Motioning for quiet, he explained his and Gail's plans to move to New Orleans in June so he could possibly locate a part-time church and she could find a teaching position. "Folks, this is a hard thing for us to do. The easiest thing would be to stay here. This is Gail's home and in many ways, has become mine. However, following God's will isn't always an easy thing to do. Abraham, Moses, and many others made enormous sacrifices in order to follow God's will. If I stayed here, I would be disobedient to God and I don't think you want a disobedient preacher." He closed by telling them he would share more about their plans in the coming weeks. "Gail and I are going to ask all of you to make an important commitment to us, and that is to pray for us every day. We are taking a journey of faith and you can be our prayer partners in this journey." Nodding to the deacon of the service, he and Gail walked to the vestibule.

He was not prepared for the tears. It seemed as if everyone who came out was crying. Some couldn't express what they wanted to say-the words just wouldn't come. So, they just hugged and cried and then cried some more. Men with wet eyes, shook his hand so hard he thought they would crush it.

Word spread quickly that he had resigned. People he hardly knew stopped him on the street to tell him how sorry they were he was leaving. He took the time to answer questions and give explanations as to why he was leaving. No need to create a situation for gossip to start. Riley Barber had advised him to be truthful and loving with people, even those who made his departure difficult.

"Mark," he said, "you'll want to come back to Gentry sometime. Make sure you leave a bridge to come back on." Another lesson from the "school of Riley."

Jimmy Deas

Chapter 19

The wedding weekend had arrived, and the usually calm Gail Smith was showing definite signs of stress. Nothing had gone wrong; everything was going according to plan and Mark could see no reason to be stressed. When he mentioned it to his mother, she responded by telling him men just didn't understand and never would. He quickly decided that silence would be the best response.

His mother had arrived on Thursday with Aunt Catherine and they were staying in Mrs. Cole's extra bedroom. Robert and his family were staying at the Smith's. He was planning to reserve a room at the motel in Tadlock for Bill and Emma Swain, which he would pay for, but Harley and Jeanette, with their servant hearts, insisted they use their spare bedroom.

Riley Barber's experience was evident at the rehearsal.

He assembled those who would have a part in the ceremony, and they rehearsed three things: when to enter, where to stand, and when to exit. It only required three simple walk-throughs, and everyone understood their role. Following the rehearsal, Mark, Gail, family, and friends went to the fellowship hall where the ladies of the church had volunteered to provide the meal. Part of their wedding gift, they had said.

The wedding was at two o'clock on Saturday so the newlyweds could drive to St. Augustine before dark. They decided to honeymoon there instead of a more exotic location and save money for the transition to New Orleans.

When the pianist began the music for Gail to enter, Mark turned to see her and was overcome. She had never been so beautiful. Her white gown gave her an angelic appearance and the glow on her face was something he hadn't seen before. When Robert gave her away and she stepped to his side, he was overcome with gratitude that God had blessed him with this special woman--the woman he wanted to spend the rest of his life with. He felt that somewhere in heaven, his father was smiling and saying, "Son, you did well."

Riley Barber's ceremony was a thing of beauty, combining the appropriate scriptures with the vows and spoken with his captivating voice. Behind him, Mark could hear women sniffing and softly blowing their noses into handkerchiefs or tissues. *Do they always do that?*

Mark and Gail departed from the church at four o'clock, giving them ample time to drive to St. Augustine.

They planned to spend four days in St. Augustine, returning home on Thursday. It seemed that every hour that passed, Mark's love for Gail increased. Walking through the Old City, strolling along the beach, or sitting in a restaurant eating, he found himself looking at her and loving her more and more.

Tuesday night, he had the nightmare. Waking up with a start, he sat up on the edge of the bed, waking up Gail. "Honey, what's wrong?" she asked. "It's the nightmare," he replied, and she could see him shaking. For the first time, she could see the effect Sammy's death had on him. She asked if he wanted to talk about it.

He was silent for a time, mulling over what Gail had said. Maybe he did need to talk about it. Stump Harris was the only other person with whom he had shared what he had discovered about Sammy's death. Maybe he needed to talk about it.

Putting their pillows against the headboard, they sat up and he proceeded to tell her about the visit with Nell Garber and reading Sammy's journal, the confrontation with Wanda

Kelly, and Stump Harris' conclusion that no evidence existed to charge her with a crime. When he finished, Gail was incredulous. "So, she gets away free after causing Sammy's death?" Nodding his head, he replied, "Honey, it looks that way."

Mark suddenly felt a sense of relief. He wasn't carrying his burden alone any longer. He pulled Gail close and hugged her. "Gail", he said, "It just doesn't make sense. Sammy wasn't in a hole and he didn't beg me to save him much less scream. The dream isn't realistic."

They sat in silence for a minute and she replied. "Honey, I'm not a dream expert but think about this. We don't know how aware Sammy of what was happening during that time. Perhaps he was aware that you were holding him as he struggled to live. And I know you would have done anything to save him."

He continued. "And I feel so idiotic about not knowing what Sammy was trying to tell me. "Ran like Joseph." I'm convinced he knew who he was talking to and tried to tell me the reason he was running. I'm a preacher, I should have understood. He was using a Bible event, trying to tell me what happened, and I failed to understand. In some ways, I feel like I failed him."

They sat quietly and then he almost whispered, "And do

I have to live with this for the rest of my life?"

"Sweetheart," she said, "I'm with you and you don't have to deal with this alone." After he fell asleep, she prayed, asking God for some relief, some resolution of this terrible thing that affected her husband. She thought that it was somewhat ironic that as he helped other people with their struggles, her husband had his own struggle. Now that she was the wife of a preacher, she was beginning to see things in a different light. She made a silent promise to minister to him and his needs as he ministered to a congregation of needs. Other than the nightmare, they enjoyed four days of honeymoon bliss.

On the ride home, Gail noticed Mark getting quieter and more introspective, causing her to ask what was wrong. "Gail, I'm worried about us moving to New Orleans." When she inquired why, he told her that he had not saved as much money as he intended. They needed enough money to live on for three to four months, until he found a part-time church and she could find a teaching position. "How much do you have saved?" she asked? He wasn't sure, maybe three hundred dollars. "And how much do we need?" she asked. "Well, a thousand dollars would get us through summer and pay for initial seminary expenses."

She leaned her head against his shoulder and said, "Then don't worry, we have enough money." Shaking his head, he asked, "What do you mean, we have enough?" "Well," she replied, "you have three hundred and I have about one thousand." Her answer left him baffled. "How did you get one thousand dollars?" She giggled and said, "I robbed a bank."

"Gail, this isn't a joking matter."

"Okay, I saved it. My living expenses aren't all that much. Mother lets me pay for half of the groceries and utilities. There is no house payment. My car is paid for. And I don't spend a lot of money on clothes and personal items. That Mr. Thomas, is how I saved a thousand dollars!" He pondered her answer and then said, "But Gail. That's your money, I can't take it."

There was a sudden change in her demeanor. She backed across the seat and her eyes flashed. Her voice had a tone he had not heard before, not even when she expressed her opinion about Wanda Kelly. "Mark Thomas let's get one thing settled right now. In this marriage, there isn't going to be any 'yours' and 'mine'. Everything is 'ours'. What's mine is yours and what's yours is mine. Isn't that the Biblical concept of marriage?" He nodded weakly, aware of where this conversation was headed and knowing he wasn't going to win. She continued. "Last Saturday, when I said, 'I do', that meant I do give you all that I am and all that I possess. Isn't that what you meant when you said, 'I do'?" Another weak nod. She relaxed, smiled, and slid back across the seat, putting her head against his shoulder. "Now, that's settled, and we can look forward to going to New Orleans." For the next half-hour, his thoughts alternated between feeling like an ungrateful jerk to knowing how blessed he was to have Gail as his wife. Whoever had said that Baptist preachers tended to marry above themselves certainly described him.

Jimmy Deas

Chapter 20

The newlyweds returned home and began packing for the move to New Orleans. Mark preached his last sermon on Sunday morning, June 13, and the church gave them a going away party that evening. As usual, there was an ample supply of food on the tables and the mood was festive, although the congregation was losing its pastor. After the meal, church members took turns expressing their goodbyes to Mark and Gail, which brought tears to her eyes and caused a lump in his throat. Harley Bass then walked to the front of the fellowship and asked Mark to join him. "Preacher, our offerings have been really good lately and we've accumulated a little money in the bank, so we have decided to invest some of our money." Mark was wondering why this topic was being discussed on this occasion. Reaching in his coat pocket, Harley pulled out an envelope and said, "Last Sunday while you were gone, we voted to invest in your education."

Handing it to Mark, he motioned for him to open it. Inside was a check for $500.00. The lump in his throat got larger and he couldn't hold back the tears. Looking around the room, he saw smiles and grins on all faces, except Gail's, who was crying. Harley told him the money was to help with his seminary expenses. When he finally regained his composure, he said, "Folks, I promise you that I will make your investment worthwhile."

Monday was packing day and they would leave on Tuesday. Mark had been perplexed about packing their belongings into two compact cars. A couple of weeks before the wedding, he stopped in Tuttle's for a soft drink and discussed his dilemma with Bob. Buck Simmons, the local handyman came in and overheard the conversation. He was a skilled carpenter and, according to the locals, could repair or build almost anything. Anyone looking at him would not have guessed he was a decorated war veteran with a box full of medals. He fought in the Battle of the Bulge and helped liberate the town of Malmedy, Belgium. On the outskirts of the small village, his unit discovered several orphans hiding in a dilapidated shed. The oldest was a girl of eighteen who caught Buck's eye immediately. Her name was Josephine, pretty with a winsome personality, and the young soldier fell in love with her. The soldiers took care of the group until Malmedy was secured and left them with the townsfolk. When the soldiers moved out, Buck gave her his address in the states and the promise that he would come back for her. She kissed him on the cheek and assured him she would wait. After the war, it took several months and an incredible amount of red tape, but Buck eventually got her to the states where they married and had three kids.

On the tenth anniversary of D-Day, a reporter from the Valdosta Daily Times wanted to do a story about Buck and his war experience. Buck declined with the simple comment, "I was just doing my job."

While drinking a cola and eating a pack of crackers, he listened to Mark and then said, "Preacher, I think I may have a solution. Let me study on it."

Two days later, Buck knocked at his door and explained his proposal. "Preacher, if you can find luggage racks to fit your cars, I can build a box, like a trunk, that will fit on top. Give y'all more space." Mark asked what it would cost. Rubbing his chin, Buck replied, "You buy the hardware and I'll build the boxes for free." Mark protested, "Buck, I can't let you do that! There's the cost of the lumber and your labor is worth something." Shaking his head, he replied, "Lumber won't cost a thing. Got plenty in my shop. As for my labor, Sammy's daddy was a friend of mine. I appreciate what you did for Nell. Consider it my way of thanking you." Mark shook his hand and thanked him. He found luggage racks in Valdosta and Buck began his project.

Early Monday morning, Buck brought the racks and boxes and mounted on the cars. Mark was impressed with the craftsmanship. Buck put flanges around the lid section so water wouldn't get in and ruin the contents if they encountered rain. Hasps and padlocks were added for security.

Ever the organizer, Gail packed their clothes in grocery bags donated by Bob Tuttle, and taped them shut, and labeled each one so they wouldn't have to search for needed items. Mark had clothes, books, and a few personal items. Gail had clothes, lots of personal items, and they had wedding gifts as well as things needed for housekeeping: pots, pans, dishes, linens.

By four o'clock, after much packing and repacking, they finally had everything packed. Both cars were stuffed tightly as well as Buck's boxes. The only empty space was the passenger seat in Gail's car where their travel suitcase and her makeup case would go. Mark was resting on the porch, drinking a glass of tea when an impulse came over him. "Mom," as he now called Mrs. Smith, "can I borrow your car?" Gail gave him a quizzical look. Kissing her on the forehead, he told her he would be back for supper. "I won't be long. Just something I need to take care of."

Ten minutes later, he was seated cross-legged on the ground next to Sammy Garber's grave. The June afternoon in the cemetery was peaceful and quiet. He could hear birds singing and somewhere in the distance, a tractor. After several minutes of silence, he talked out loud as if he and Sammy were having a conversation.

"Sammy, I found your journal and I know what happened that night. I can't begin to tell you how much I admire your commitment to do the right thing and not compromise what you believed. You may have lost your life, but you kept your integrity. I confronted Wanda but she denied what she did, and unfortunately, we can't prove anything. Your mom is doing better, and I think she will be okay. She loved you so much and misses you greatly. I guess our lives will always be connected as I was the last person you spoke to before you died. Sammy, believe me when I say, I wish I could have done something to keep you alive." He paused to gather his thoughts. "Sammy, I don't know why God chose to take you from us. As the old hymn says, *'We'll understand it better by and by.'* The Bible says that to be absent from the body is to be present with the Lord, so I know you are with Jesus." Rising to one knee, he placed a hand on top of the headstone and reflected on the words and dates etched into the granite. How ironic that the date of birth and date of death was separated by a hyphen, literally, a dash. No matter the length of life, that's what was put on a grave marker. Ironic, yet appropriate because even at its longest, life was short and, in Sammy's case, death was so unpredictable. Life, a dash! God put those verses in the Bible, comparing life to a vapor or a flower that lives briefly and then wilts, to keep us aware of that fact. Sammy Garber's life was certainly brief. "Sammy, I will see you in heaven," he said softly. As he sat by the grave, a peace settled over him, unlike anything he had known.

Standing, he dusted his pants, took one last look at the grave and walked back to the car. He didn't know it then, but there would be no more nightmares. He would always remember Sammy Garber, but not because of a bad dream.

Ran Like Joseph

ABOUT THE AUTHOR

Jimmy Deas is a retired Baptist pastor who lives in Live Oak, Florida.
He and his wife Sherry have two daughters and three grandchildren.
He grew up in the North Florida towns of Lee, Madison, Greenville,
and Jennings.
Dr. Deas holds degrees from North Florida Community College and
Luther Rice Seminary.

He is the author of A Teacher's Gift and Other Stories, Just a Dog
and Other Stories, The Jonah Trait, Just Have Faith, and Prodigal
Sons. He can be contacted at drjdeas@icloud.com